Daniel
and the
Black Horned Buck

By

Marvin D. Braun

This book is a work of fiction. Places, events, and situations in this story are purely fictional. Any resemblance to actual persons, living or dead, is coincidental.

© 2003, 2004 by Marvin D. Braun. All rights reserved.

No part of this book may be reproduced, stored in a retrieval system, or transmitted by any means, electronic, mechanical, photocopying, recording, or otherwise, without written permission from the author.

ISBN: 1-4140-3900-X (e-book)
ISBN: 1-4140-3898-4 (Paperback)
ISBN: 1-4140-3899-2 (Dust Jacket)

This book is printed on acid free paper.

For information about other hunting books by Marvin Braun go to:

http://www.danielsfirstdeerhunt.com

1stBooks - rev. 12/09/03

This book is dedicated to Dale. My brothers and I hunted with Dale in the Black Hills for over 15 years. He taught us many helpful things about deer hunting and life. Dale was one of the funniest people I have ever had the privilege to spend time with. He was also an exceptionally good deer hunter, and one of the toughest guys I've ever had to follow up a mountain.

Dale joined us briefly at our Black Hills deer camp on November 5, 1999. The following evening, he succumbed to a long, hard battle with cancer. We like to think that he just climbed that final mountain a few years ahead of us. We miss you, buddy, but we know we'll see you later.

Marvin Braun

7/28/01

Table of Contents

Chapter 1	Doughnuts	1
Chapter 2	The Black-Horned Buck	12
Chapter 3	Guns and Ammo	23
Chapter 4	Double Buck Ridge	34
Chapter 5	The Great Pickle Lift	45
Chapter 6	Potato Pool	57
Chapter 7	Snow	66

Chapter 8	The Strip	75
Chapter 9	Arrow Heads	89
Chapter 10	Respirator Ridge	102
Chapter 11	Old Blackie	110
Chapter 12	The Big Old Ugly	123
Chapter 13	The Surprise	135

Chapter 1
Doughnuts

The sign said:

Have you dug

Wall Drug

"Do they really give hunters free doughnuts at the Wall Drug restaurant?" Daniel asked.

"They sure do." answered Father. "We stop every year."

"Yeah, but if you want the waitress to give you one with frosting, and not just a plain one, you gotta be as good-looking as me." Todd added, laughing loudly at his own joke and readjusting his cowboy hat.

Todd was Daniel's cousin. Todd was always a lot of fun and Daniel liked him a lot, even if he was quite a few years older.

"If that's true, Todd," Uncle Ron kidded, "then how come they gave Old Blue a frosted doughnut the year I brought him along?" Old Blue was one of Ron's coon hounds. Everyone laughed loudly, even Todd.

It was the last day of October and they were on their way to the Black Hills for their annual deer hunt. Every year Daniel's father and his three brothers rented a cabin in the Black Hills. They stayed for several days hunting, playing cards, and having fun. This was the first year that Daniel got to go along. He was really looking forward to it, but knew he'd get teased a lot by his uncles.

As usual, he and Father had spent a lot of time target shooting and getting ready for the hunt.

"Hunting deer in the Black Hills is a lot different than hunting deer on Uncle Ted's ranch," Father told him. "We always see deer, but you've got to make sure they have at least two points on each side before you can shoot. Often, you get just a glimpse of a deer through the trees, and it's hard to tell how big their 'rack' is, or if they have antlers at all. Sometimes, the branches of a tree look like the deer's antlers. You have to be real sure before you shoot. That's one of the things that makes it such a challenge."

Whenever Father talked about hunting, you could see his excitement. One day when Daniel, his younger brother Dougy, and Father were out scouting for deer on Ted's ranch, Dougy mentioned it.

"Hey Dad," he asked, "how come whenever you talk about deer and stuff, you talk louder and your eyes get bigger?" All three of them laughed.

"Do I really do that?" Father asked. Both boys nodded. Father chuckled again and added, "I guess I love to hunt and fish so much, that whenever I talk about it, I get excited." Then he reached over and rumpled Dougy's hair. "Thanks for noticing Dougy, I can always count on you for a laugh."

Wall Drug was really a neat place. They had old antique guns hanging all over the restaurant. Also,

Marvin D. Braun

there were hundreds of Western paintings to look at. Daniel especially enjoyed looking at the knives. Many were handmade out of deer or elk antlers. Mother had bought one for Father a few years ago as a Christmas present. Daniel had helped her pick it out. Father still used it every year for deer hunting.

As they passed the life-sized cement dinosaur on their way into Wall, Daniel was sorry to see that there was a fence around it now. He could remember when you could walk right up to it and climb on it. His parents had a picture of Daniel, Dougy, and their older sister, Angie, sitting on the dinosaur's tail. He could understand why they had to fence it off, though. Otherwise, some dumb kid like Dougy would climb all the way to the dinosaur's head and fall off and get hurt.

The trip so far had been a lot of fun. Much of the talk was about hunting or about some of the things that had happened on previous trips.

"Do you guys remember the time we tied those great big old antlers on the head of that scrawny little buck?" Uncle Ted asked. Uncle Ron and Father chuckled and nodded in agreement. Daniel and Todd listened carefully to hear the whole story.

Ted continued, "One year somebody found a real nice set of antlers, that a buck had shed. All the bucks we got that season were small. We tied the big rack we had found, onto the head of one of the small bucks when we put it on top of the vehicle to haul home."

Ron added, "Whenever we stopped to get gas or eat, you should have seen people look at that deer. They must have thought we were quite the hunters...until they went for a closer look and saw the antlers were tied on!"

Some of the talk was very serious also. "I'm glad we don't hunt California Gulch anymore." Father commented. "It was getting too crowded and too dangerous."

"How come, Dad?" Daniel asked.

"Well, the last time we hunted it, your Uncle Marlin and I were sitting on a hill overlooking a large brush patch. Two hunters, whom we didn't know, walked out on a ridge across the canyon and emptied their rifles into that patch of brush. They hoped to flush out any deer that might have been hiding there."

"What if a hunter would have been in there?"

"That's a good question Dan. I don't want to be around hunters that are that stupid. We haven't hunted in that area since."

As they parked their vehicle in front of the world-famous Wall Drug Store, Daniel asked, "Dad, do you remember the time we lost Dougy here?"

"I sure do, that was pretty scary."

"What happened?" Ted questioned.

"It was several summers ago when Dougy was only four. We were in the back courtyard looking at the stuffed animals, and all of a sudden, Dougy was gone!"

"Where did he go?"

"Well, the place was packed with tourists, and Wall Drug is a big place. I had Grandma stay at the back door and I watched the front doors while his mother searched the place. Guess where she found him?"

"With Dougy, I can't imagine," Ron answered.

"He was right up front watching the automated cowboys playing."

"No!"

"Yup. When his mother found him, he had his nose right up against the glass. She was in a panic and asked him, 'Dougy what are you doing here? We've been looking all over for you.' He acted somewhat offended by our lack of trust and said, 'Well, Mom, you know I was just wookin' at the towboys.' They all chuckled at the story and Father added, "After that we've kept closer track of Dougy."

By now, they were in the store and made their way to the back where the restaurant was located. The hostess seated them and commented, "You guys must be hunters."

"We try to be," Todd answered.

"How about a free doughnut?"

"Sounds good, thanks."

"Just go up to the counter over there and tell them you're hunters and they'll give you your doughnut. Help yourself to the free ice water and the five cent coffee, too."

Marvin D. Braun

When they were finished they bought a dozen doughnuts with maple frosting and a dozen with chocolate to take to the cabin.

"I need to stop at the camping store," Father commented. "Shall we meet at the suburban in fifteen minutes?" The others murmured their agreement and moved off in different directions. Daniel and father went to the camping store.

"What do you want to get, Dad?" Daniel asked.

"I want to get each of us one of those magnesium fire starters for our survival kits."

"How come, Dad? We already have matches."

"I know Daniel. But, have you ever tried to start a fire using damp wood or kindling with just matches?" Daniel nodded, so Father continued, "The way these magnesium fire starters work is, you scrape off a few shavings with your knife, cover them with kindling, and then light the magnesium chips. They start right up and burn at a temperature of 5,400 degrees. Magnesium burns so hot, it even lights wet kindling."

"Cool."

The camping store was full of all kinds of neat stuff. On one wall there were old guns for sale. There were many different pistols and rifles that the gunfighters of the old West had used including a fifty caliber Sharp's buffalo rifle, the kind Buffalo Bill Cody had used.

"How come they're so cheap?" Daniel asked.

"Because they're just replicas, Dan. They look like the real guns, but they don't shoot. They sure would be nice hanging over a fireplace wouldn't they?"

"They sure would," Daniel agreed.

"Well, it's time to go. We're a little late, the others will probably be waiting for us."

As they hurried out to the vehicle, they passed through Wall Drug's Statue Alley. Statue Alley was a wide corridor that had stores and gift shops on both sides. In the corridor itself, were a number of different, realistic, life-sized statues. As they rushed past a statue of a cowboy with his arm around Annie Oakley, the cowboy said, "Boo!"

Both Daniel and his father were startled, but as Todd's unmistakable laugh filled the corridor, they had to laugh at the joke themselves.

When Todd was done laughing he explained. "I stopped in one of the stores, and looked at their cowboy hats. I was hurrying along because I thought I was late, when I noticed you two were still in the camping store. I knew you'd be coming this way shortly so I just thought I'd rest right here beside old Annie. Surprised ya good, didn't I?" He laughed some more, slapping his leg with his cowboy hat.

Uncle Ted and Uncle Ron were waiting by the suburban when they got there. They each were munching on a frosted doughnut. They piled into the vehicle and headed west on the interstate. Several miles to the south, Daniel could see parts of the Badlands. Their jagged peaks reminded him of the Disneyland castle.

Suddenly, Todd and Ron slid together, trapping Daniel between them.

"It's sixty-five miles to the cabin," Uncle Ron explained. "I expect by that time, we'll know about all your girlfriends." And with that, the tickling began.

Daniel and the Black Horned Buck

As they passed the life-sized dinosaur, Daniel was sorry to see that there was a fence around it now.

Chapter 2

The Black-Horned Buck

Fortunately, the tickling didn't last for long. Soon, the talk turned to the Black- Horned Buck. Several years ago, Bob, one of the guys who hunted with the group in the Black Hills, claimed to have spotted a very unusual buck.

"The thing is," Bob had explained, "not only is this buck big, but his antlers aren't gray or ivory like most other deer's racks, they're black."

Daniel and the Black Horned Buck

The next season Daniel's father had confirmed Bob's story. He was blocking for a drive, when he spotted the unusual buck. Blocking meant that he was waiting at the end of an area that the other hunters were walking through. The idea of a drive is for some hunters to sneak into position and remain quiet while the other hunters "drive" the deer towards the blockers, giving them a good opportunity to harvest a deer.

Bob had placed the blockers in locations where he felt they could effectively see most deer trying to escape. He had positioned Dick, Daniel's father, on a large rock beside one of the well-traveled deer trails. Father explained what had happened.

"I was sitting on this flat, black, rock, when suddenly I saw, not heard, this buck sneaking through the trees. He made no sound, even though the ground was covered with dry leaves and pine needles. I pulled up my rifle and barely got my scope on him when he just melted away into the brush like a gray ghost. He was a big buck, but the strange thing was his antlers; they looked black, not gray like other buck's antlers. Actually, they were about the same color as the rock I was sitting on. I knew then, that I had just blown my chance at bagging the Big Black-Horned Buck that Bob had told us about. Since then, we've called that rock, Big Black Buck Rock. That drive is one of my favorite hunts."

"Mine, too," Todd added, "but it's also one of the toughest climbs for the walkers. Before you start down Big Black Buck Draw, you have to climb Respirator Ridge, and that is one long, steep climb."

"Yes, and if you're the poor sucker who has to walk that big rocky mound right in the middle, then it's really a tough drive."

"It's worth it, though. When you finally reach the top and break through the trees on the other side of Respirator Ridge, the view is fantastic. It reminds me of that movie <u>The Lost Valley</u>."

The hunters named most of the drives, hills, ridges, and landmarks that they hunted. This made it easier to talk about and identify when they hunted the same spots later. Since it was Daniel's first time to hunt in the Black Hills, most of the names were new to him, names like: The 385 Strip, Deer Heaven Draw, Green Shack Drive, Lost Todd Wilderness, Big Ugly Hill, Novotny's Knob and The High Pocket.

Father explained, "The names get changed occasionally, especially if something significant happens that makes it easier for everyone to remember. Like Lost Todd Wilderness; we all remember waiting and searching for Todd. So, when someone says, 'Let's hunt Lost Todd Wilderness,' we all know where they mean..."

Todd interrupted him. "Yeah, right, everyone except me. I still don't know my way around up there." Everyone laughed as Todd continued, "That's just great. The first year I go hunting up here, and I just happen to get lost for an hour or so, and you name a whole forest after me!"

"Just be glad," Ron added, "that they didn't change the name of The Big Ugly Hill to The Big Ugly Todd!" They all laughed again.

"Has anyone else ever seen the Black-Horned Buck, Dad?" Daniel asked.

"I'm not sure. Todd, do you recall anyone else seeing Big Blacky?"

"No, all I remember seeing is a lot of trees and rocks, and they all looked the same to me. Besides, I was nearly unconscious by the time I had climbed to the top of Respirator Ridge. Next time, I'm going to take some oxygen along so I have something to revive me once I reach the summit." He chuckled at his own joke.

Father continued, "As far as we know Daniel, the buck's still around. At least, no one in our group harvested him."

"His antlers would make a neat wall mount, wouldn't they, Dad?"

"They sure would, especially if his horns are as black as I remember them."

"What do you think would make a buck's rack that dark?"

"I'm not sure. That's something we should ask Mr. Ludkey, the game warden. I would guess, it's either genetic, he inherited that trait from his father, or, it's because he's eating something that has a lot of a certain kind of mineral in it, like iron. Maybe, the same mineral that makes Big Black Rock look so black."

"How can you keep from getting lost," Daniel asked, "especially when you're on an unfamiliar drive?"

"You want me to answer that?" Todd hooted, then he continued seriously. "The first thing, is to trust your compass. I can remember when I was lost, I thought it was broken. When you get lost, your directions get all turned around. You think your compass isn't working. Before you even begin the drive, take a bearing with your compass of the direction you need to go, then stick to it."

"Good advice, Todd. Bob and Dale are good at picking out drives for us that are fairly simple, or at least they try to. What I mean is, they try to pick out spots where the end of the drive is a road, a creek or a fence. If you walk in the direction you're supposed to, and stop when you reach the creek or logging road, most of the time you'll be okay."

"And the rest of the time, they'll find you a few days later, like they did me," Todd joked again.

"You could just stay with us in the cabin, Daniel," Ron suggested.

"Yes, that would be much safer," Ted continued the ribbing. "You could help us cook, play cards, and safe stuff like that."

Daniel's uncles Ron and Ted loved to kid him. Every year they went along for the Black Hills deer hunt, but they never hunted. They did most of the cooking for the other hunters, and during the rest of the day, they went to pawn shops, flea markets, etc.

Uncle Ron hunted at home in Nebraska, but didn't care to spend the $135 dollars it cost for an out-of-state deer license. Besides, he liked spending time with Ted. Uncle Ted had some of the best hunting land in the world, and yet he rarely hunted. Both were content to help out around the cabin and let the others hunt.

"Look, there's an antelope!" Todd pointed at an antelope standing out in a wheat field next to the interstate.

As they observed the prong horn, Uncle Ron spoke. "Okay, here's a trivia question for you. Buck deer lose their antlers every winter around February. What about antelope, do they shed their horns every winter like deer?"

Daniel loved this part of the trip. Every so often, someone would ask a question about hunting or wildlife. It was fun to try and stump the others.

Everyone made their guesses. "What's the right answer, Uncle Ron?" Daniel asked.

"There's a difference between horns and antlers. <u>Horns</u> grow a little bit each year and they're not shed every winter like antlers. Antelope grow horns, deer grow antlers. Therefore, a prong horn antelope does not shed his <u>horns</u>, only animals who grow <u>antlers</u> shed them every year."

"There's a B1 bomber, Daniel!" Father pointed up into the sky. Ellsworth Air Force Base was located near Rapid City. A squadron of the B1B's were stationed there. Training flights were often visible from the interstate, especially their takeoffs and landings.

As the huge black jet crossed the interstate in front of them, Daniel could see the distinctive hooked beak

Marvin D. Braun

of the B1 B. The jet reminded him of a large predatory bird going after its prey.

They passed through Rapid City and began their ascent into the Black Hills. Daniel remembered from history class that the native Indians had named the hills Paha Sapa or Black Hills, because, from the distance of the prairie, the pine forests that covered the low mountains looked black. Right now, the hills were speckled with white because of snow. He wondered what the Lakota words for white hills were.

They spotted several whitetail doe next to the road, but no bucks. As they crossed Pactola Dam, Daniel knew they were getting close to the cabin. Several miles farther and they pulled into the steep driveway. There were fewer trees surrounding the house than Daniel had remembered, but that was because a forest fire had very nearly destroyed the cabin two summers ago.

Uncle Marlin's jeep was already parked in front of the cabin, so he and Spence had beat them here. Spence was a good friend who lived in Bozeman, Montana. Uncle Marlin lived in Livingston, Montana.

The two of them traveled the the long trip to South Dakota together for the annual deer hunt.

As Father stopped the vehicle, Marlin and Spence both stepped out onto the second floor balcony and let out a cheer. Uncle Marlin reminded Daniel of Theodore Roosevelt when he was in his Rough Rider uniform, with his heavy mustache, high boots, suspenders and neckerchief.

"Hello," he shouted from the balcony. Then, holding his hat aloft in the air he added, "Let this year's hunt officially begin!"

Marvin D. Braun

Uncle Marlin reminded Daniel of Theodore Roosevelt with his heavy mustache, high boots, suspenders and neckerchief.

Chapter 3
Guns and Ammo

Daniel's feet came off the ground as Uncle Marlin lifted him up, swung him around in a circle, and gave him a huge bear hug.

"Good to see you, Dan," he said gruffly. "We'll do our best to make a man out of you this weekend." He laughed as he set Daniel back down.

Next, it was Spence's turn. He also gave Daniel a hug as he asked, "How ya doing, Bud?" Spence had been a good friend of the family ever since doing his chiropractic internship with Daniel's father.

"I've got to tell you," Father spoke, "the last thing his mother said to me before we left was this, 'Dick, you promise me that you won't let all those men corrupt my little boy.'"

Spence, Todd and Marlin all laughed. Daniel was slightly embarrassed that his mother still called him her little boy. As soon as they had gotten into the suburban, he had asked, "Dad, what does corrupt mean?"

Father chuckled. "It means that you might hear a naughty word or two at deer camp that you shouldn't ever use, but especially not in front of your mother."

Marlin and Spence also greeted the rest of the hunters.

"Nice growth, Dick," Spence commented on Father's new beard. "It looks cool."

"Thanks," Father responded. "Yours looks good, too."

"What about mine?" Ron asked. Uncle Ron had worn a beard for so many years that everyone was used to it. Since he rarely trimmed it, he looked rather 'scraggly'. He was also a big guy; six feet two inches tall and 250 pounds.

"Let me give you a little advice, big brother," Marlin answered. "If I were you, I wouldn't go into the woods looking like that, or somebody will mistake you for a bear and shoot you." The group laughed.

"Come on, let's get this stuff unloaded so we can do some hunting," Father suggested. "Who else is coming this afternoon?"

Marlin answered, "Just Kendall and Robert. Dale, Clyde, and Lee had to work this afternoon, but they'll be here at 5:30 tomorrow morning."

"I have a suggestion," Todd offered. "Since it is the cold and flu season, maybe we should postpone the morning's hunt until 8:00 or so, you know, until I'm better rested." Everyone groaned as Todd enjoyed his own joke.

All pitched in and unloaded the groceries, clothes, rifles, and ammunition packed into the suburban. The amount of food was awesome!

There was a pile on the kitchen counter for candy, one for chips, another for cookies, cakes and pies. There was still another pile of bread, lunch meat, vegetables, and jerky. The refrigerator freezer was full of delicious elk steak and moose roasts that Marlin and Spence had brought from Montana. Uncle Ted had brought some of his homemade deer bologna.

Uncle Ron placed several mysterious packages of frozen meat into the freezer that he wouldn't identify.

"I'm going to make you guess what kind of meat this is," he stated.

It took them about an hour to get all their stuff unpacked and organized.

The cabin that they rented every year wasn't really a cabin at all. Actually, it was a very nice house that they rented from Uncle Marlin's friend. Daniel especially liked the huge deck that went around two sides of the house and gave you a great view of the Black Hills. Father had told Daniel that during previous years, they could have shot deer from the deck. They never had, though.

"Now, where's that new firearm I've been hearing so much about?" Marlin asked Daniel.

It was true, Daniel had bought himself a different rifle. He had traded in his lever action Browning .243 for a Browning bolt action 7 mm .08.

"I'll show you, Uncle Marlin." He led Marlin downstairs and unlatched the gun case. He opened the rifle's bolt to make sure it was unloaded, and then carefully handed it to his uncle.

"Whoooeee," Marlin whistled, "this looks nice." He held it up to his shoulder and looked through the scope. "It pulls up real nice, too. Did it come this length?"

"No, Dad and I cut off the stock about one inch." Daniel, Father and Marlin all had short arms. For that reason, they either bought guns with short stocks, or cut the stocks off so that they fit right.

"You did a nice job. I was a little worried that your .243 wouldn't be enough fire power for the big stuff like elk. How did you decide on a 7 mm .08?"

Daniel and his father had spent a lot of time researching what caliber of rifle to get. It had been fun looking at the ballistic charts on all the different rifles. Most deer hunting experts didn't feel that a .243 was big enough, even for deer, so they suggested a caliber bigger than a .243. On the other hand, if you went with one of the large calibers, often they had considerable recoil or kick, especially for someone Daniel's size.

"We looked at a lot of different rifles, Uncle Marlin. We decided on the 7 mm .08 for three reasons: First, it has low recoil. Second, you can reload shells from 120 grain bullets clear up to 175 grains…

"That's great!" Marlin interrupted. "That means you can use it on elk next year when you finally come out to Montana to hunt. What was the third reason?"

"You know in the reloading books they talk about a bullet's *sectional density* and its *ballistic coefficient*."

"Yes, I've heard of them, but I don't really understand them."

"Well, anyway, the 7 mm .08, for its size, beats almost everything else. If you want to know more about that stuff, you'll have to ask Dad."

Daniel and the Black Horned Buck

Father, who had been listening to the conversation offered, "Very simply, the higher a bullet's ballistic coefficient, the easier it flies through the air. Sectional density helps determine the B.C. or ballistic coefficient. You got it, Marly?" He slapped his brother jokingly on the back and gave him another hug. "It sure is good to be here. I look forward to this trip all year."

"Me, too. Hey, Dan," he handed the rifle back to Daniel. "That sure is a dandy gun. Your dad said you bought this with your own money. How come you're so rich?"

Daniel laughed. "I wouldn't consider myself rich, Uncle Marlin. I earned the money working for Emil. Dad said you used to work for him, too."

"Yeah, that was when he ran the gas station. What's he doing now?"

"He farms and raises a few cattle. Plus, he mows grass for people. I got to help with all sorts of stuff like fixing fence, chopping musk thistles, fixing machinery, and running the lawn mower. He even let me drive his new pickup."

"What a deal. When you get home, ask him if he has a job for me, too. I need a new rifle."

"Me, too", said Todd. "A man just can't have too many rifles. You know, I'm a little worried that we don't have enough food either." Once again, he guffawed at his own joke.

Just then, a white pickup drove up the driveway. They all headed out onto the deck to see who it was. It was Robert and Kendall.

Robert was first to speak as he got out of his vehicle. "Afternoon, boys!" Then in a fake southern drawl he continued, "She's a real purty day, ain't she?"

"Robert, if I were you," Kendall warned, "I'd protect your face. These boys have been known to put out an eye or two from that balcony."

The whole group laughed uproariously. It was almost true. Several years ago, one of Spence's friends had thrown a snowball at the men standing on the deck. In the "exchange of fire," a snowball had struck him in the eye. The eye had immediately swollen shut. Fortunately, it was just scratched and not permanently injured, but the incident had never been forgotten.

By now, Robert, whose nickname was 'Old Bob,' and Kendall, whose nickname was Rusty, had climbed the stairs. Everyone greeted each other happily. The annual Black Hills deer hunt was actually a reunion of old friends. Most of the group had known each other and hunted together for many years.

Father had told Daniel, "Whether I get a deer or not in the Black Hills really doesn't matter, the funnest part is spending time with friends and family."

The group continued to chat happily as they got dressed in their hunting clothes.

"Although it's not a competition," Father had told Daniel, "it's always interesting to see what new hunting clothing or equipment everyone is wearing. In a way, each one does try to out do the other. Sometimes, the new stuff doesn't show up until later in the hunt. Like, when someone pulls out a new hunting knife as they're ready to field-dress the deer, or a new set of binoculars, or a new compass. Usually, your

Uncle Marlin wins. He always seems to have a new gadget or two that we've never seen before."

Getting dressed didn't take as long as usual because the weather was so warm. When all who were hunting were ready, they merged in front of the cabin and discussed where to hunt. They decided to make a drive along a huge ridge located behind the cabin that they had named Novotny's Knob. Robert, who was considered the *Hunt master*, gave the instructions.

Daniel knew that the group joked about the position of Hunt master. But, Father had explained to him how important it was for one person to actually take charge and coordinate the hunt.

"For any drive to be successful and safe, people have to be in the right position at the right time. It works best if one person gives the instructions. Robert does a great job because he knows the layout of the terrain better than anyone else in the group, except, of course, Dale." Dale was a friend of Roberts' and had hunted with the group for fifteen years.

Daniel and the Black Horned Buck

As Robert continued to explain the drive, and tell the hunters their positions, Todd moaned, "You mean I get to climb Heart Break Ridge again this year?"

"That's right," Robert replied. "We need an ex-Marine to do the tough jobs."

"Well, then, let's do it." They all began getting into their designated vehicles.

Todd had been in the Marines until he had been injured during training. Daniel thought he still looked like a Marine in his red-colored head bandana and army fatigues.

Just as the vehicles were taking off, Todd stuck his head out the window and shouted one last bit of encouragement to the other hunters. "Come on you devil dogs, let's go take that ridge."

Chapter 4

Double Buck Ridge

Bob dropped Daniel and his father off beside an old logging trail. The road had been so rough, that Daniel's head had nearly hit the roof of the pickup several times as they bounced across ruts and rocks that jutted up out of the ground.

As Bob drove away to organize the others hunters, father began moving slowly across a grassy meadow. It was a beautiful spot with tall pine trees dotting the clearing. Straight ahead, but several miles away, was the Seth Bullock fire watch tower. To their right was the huge rocky peak the hunters had named Novotny's Knob. To their left, was an even higher hill. The hillside facing them was almost barren of trees, which made it a good place to spot deer and block for a drive.

"That," father stopped to rest and explain, "is the famous Double Buck Ridge. We named it that, because two years ago, we bagged two nice bucks on the same drive. Last year, they drove two bull elk by me. The one was only thirty yards from me for about ten minutes, he never knew I was there. So, be careful, Dan. Don't mistake an elk for a great big dear."

"How do I tell the difference?"

"You'll know. Elk are much larger than deer, plus they're darker brown in color. Also, they have a mane around their neck, kind of like a lion."

They continued moving towards a pile of rocks several hundred yards ahead. Although they tried to be as quiet as possible, it was difficult because their path was littered with fallen and partially burned pine trees from an old forest fire.

"How do you know where to sit dad?"

"It's hard to know Daniel. The main thing is to try and find a place where you have a good field-of-fire. Up by those rocks, you can see pretty good in all directions. Also, I've been on this particular drive enough times to know that the deer come right by this spot."

It took them a few more minutes to reach the rocks and find a suitable place to sit.

"This is where all our target practice pays off, Dan. From this spot, most shots would be one-hundred to three-hundred yards."

"I'm not sure I could hit a deer three-hundred yards away, Dad. That's three football fields."

"Some guys take shots like that all the time. I prefer a closer shot myself. One thing though, if you are going to shoot that far, the deer should be standing still. Also, you need to rest your rifle on something like a log or branch to make sure you're steady when you shoot. A hunter's goal should always be to harvest an animal with one properly placed shot."

Their attention was drawn to a flurry of movement in a pile of rocks just next to them.

"What is that Dad?"

"It's a chipmunk. They're all over the place in the Black Hills. They look a lot like a gopher, don't they?" Daniel nodded in agreement as they quietly watched the tiny rodent stop right next to Daniel's shoe. Suddenly, it must have realized they were people. It gave a frightened little squeak and scurried off across the rocks.

"Dougy would sure like one of those for a pet wouldn't he Dad?"

"He sure would, but I doubt if the poor chipmunk would last even one day between Dougy and the cat." They both chuckled softly.

"Yeah, he'd probably try to dress it in some of Angie's Barbie Doll clothes." Angie was Daniel and Doug's older sister.

Father nodded and said, "That Dougy, what would we laugh about without him."

Marvin D. Braun

Daniel smiled and shrugged his shoulders. Dougy was a funny kid without even trying to be. Just last weekend Daniel and his father had gone scouting on Ted's ranch. Uncle Ted had some great deer hunting land. While scouting, they had discovered a dead three-point buck. When they got home, Father had called Mr. Ludke, the game warden, and told him about it. After examining the dead deer, Mr. Ludke had called back and reported to him that the deer had died of hemorrhagic disease.

As father began explaining to Daniel what the warden had said, Dougy strolled into the room; he looked mad. He listened quietly for a little bit and then complained, "Dad, Angie just slapped me on the hinder really hard for no good reason. If she don't stop right now, I'm going to give <u>her</u> that 'hinder-agic' disease!"

When they were all done laughing, father continued telling Daniel what Mr. Ludke had said. "It's killed quit a few whitetails this fall. It's spread by certain insects. Fortunately, it generally just affects whitetails and not muleys. I sure would hate to see all the muley deer die on Ted's ranch."

"So that hill is the famous Novotny's Knob." Daniel pointed to the rocky ridge just to their right.

"Yup, it may not look like much from here, but when you get up on top, it's brutal. There are rocks and fallen trees all over. It's like finding your way through an obstacle course. It always amazes me that you'll find deer sign in the most rugged places - in the steepest places and between rock crevices and all sorts of places like that. I guess we need to understand that deer can get around in these hills much better than we can."

"They're smarter than we give them credit for too, aren't they."

"They sure are. Remember those pictures in my hunting magazine, where that buck was sneaking away from those hunters by crawling on its belly down a dry creek bed. It makes you wonder how many times they play hide-and-seek with you."

"This would be an awesome place to play hide-and-seek. Only thing, I might not be able to find myself." They both laughed quietly.

Father pointed to their left. "That's the slope the other guys are walking right now. The far side of that is the hill we call Heart Break Hill. That's the one Todd loves to climb so much. He glanced at his watch. "We could start seeing deer real soon. The trick is being able to see if they have antlers amongst all the pine trees."

They watched the forest-covered side-hill in front of them in silence for several minutes before Daniel felt his father's body stiffen. "Here they come," He whispered excitedly.

Daniel looked in the direction he was looking. At first, he didn't see anything but trees, but then he saw movement. A moment later two does and a fawn broke out of the woods and into the clearing. They stopped and looked back in the direction they had just come.

"I imagine our hunters spooked them this way," father whispered, "They're going to come right by us.

Make sure you hold real still, and they probably won't even know we're here, especially since the wind is caring our scent away from them."

Both adult deer studied the woods behind them nervously. Daniel could see their noses twitching as they tried to pick up the scent of whatever had spooked them out of their beds. Suddenly, the largest of the does stamped her foot on the ground and snorted loudly. To Daniel, it sounded just like she was blowing air out of her nose. Then their whitetails flew up and they began bounding up the path right in front of Daniel and his father.

Father whispered again, "Whenever they do that, they've smelled you. One of our walkers must be getting close."

"Sure wished one of them had horns," Daniel whispered back as the does passed by. "That would've been an easy shot." He noticed that the one deer had her mouth open. When they were out of sight, he asked, "Why did that deer have her mouth open?"

"I'm not real sure, Dan. I've seen deer do that lots of times. I always thought it was because they were tired and just short of breath."

"My mouth would be open too, if I ran as far up this hill as they did. Only, it'd be open because I was puking!"

They both laughed as father added, "If you could run like that, Coach Whaler would really like you on the track team."

Daniel nodded and then asked, "Dad, back on Ted's ranch where we deer hunt, we can see a lot farther and we're more familiar with the land. But here, even if I did see a buck coming in the trees, how would I know that I wouldn't be shooting right at one of the walkers?"

"It really is hard to know Dan. All I can tell you is that you've got to be very careful, and if you're not sure where that bullet is going to end up, then don't shoot."

"There's one of the guys now." He pointed towards the top of the hill. Daniel could just barely make out a splotch of blaze orange clear up the hill just on the edge of the trees. The hunter stopped for a few seconds until he apparently spotted them. He waved his arm in greeting, until Daniel waved back. Then he began carefully moving down the rocky hillside.

"That's Bob. He always takes the top of the ridge on this drive."

"He's kinda hard to see."

"I agree. All the color he's wearing is a blaze orange cap, which is all that is required by law. Myself, I like to wear more orange than that. I think it's safer because people can see you much better."

Soon, they detected several other hunters coming out of the trees. It took them a lot longer to reach Daniel and his father than it had the three deer that they had spotted a few minutes before.

As the guys began arriving, the same questions were asked over and over: "Did you see any?" "How about any with horns?" "Did anybody see any nice ones?" When all the walkers were accounted for, they all headed back to the pickup, the whole group, chatting happily.

Todd fell into step beside Daniel. Suddenly, he stopped and grabbed Daniel's arm. "Shhh," he said softly, "I think I hear something." His face was very serious. Daniel stopped also and listened intently to see if he could hear what Todd was hearing. A loud farting noise escaped from Todd's backside. Before Daniel could say anything, his cousin spoke again, "Yup, I was right, the great muley buck has just spoken!" He slapped Daniel on the back and began moving toward the vehicle, guffawing loudly.

Chapter 5
The Great Pickle Lift

After they did one more drive, which was unsuccessful, Robert made the decision to quit for the day. "Well, boys," he said, "it's going to be dark in forty-five minutes or so. Since I don't want to get any of you green horns lost this late in the day, and then have to spend most of my night searching for your mangy carcasses, I suggest we do a little road hunting on our way back to the cabin. Besides, I can't wait to try that mystery meal that Ron promised he was making for supper."

It was true, Ron had been very careful to keep the contents of several packages of meat concealed from them. He promised that he and Ted would have a delicious feast of the mystery meat when they returned for supper.

When they drove up the steep driveway to the cabin, there was another pickup parked in front. As the hunters climbed out of their vehicles, Robert announced, "Dale must be here."

Father said to Daniel, "You've never met Dale have you, Son?" Daniel shook his head no. "Well then, you're in for a treat. This guy is one of the funniest and craziest guys I know. He's also one of the toughest, cagiest deer hunters you'll ever meet."

"What do you mean?"

"I expect you'll find out tomorrow."

The hunters unloaded their rifles and took off their hunting caps and coats on the first floor of the cabin. Much of it was laid on the pool table situated in the middle of the room.

Suddenly, a voice Daniel had never heard before, cried out, "What have you done to my potato pool table? "Everyone burst out laughing. Daniel looked up to see a man coming down the hallway with a bag of chips in his hands.

Daniel recalled Father telling him about an incident several years ago. There was one pool ball missing. Instead of playing without it, Dale grabbed a potato from a sack sitting nearby and insisted they play 'potato pool'. The potato wasn't completely round, so it made it a very unusual game. Since that time, every year at the cabin, they had a 'potato pool' tournament.

All the men greeted and hugged Dale warmly. He began examining the hunter's hands.

"I don't see any blood on anybody's hands," he commented. "I suppose the master is going to have to show you how it's done tomorrow." He continued to dig into the bag of corn chips and stuff them into his mouth. His voice seemed very sincere as he got to Robert and remarked, "I'm very disappointed in you, Robert. All of these years of training and you're still such a novice." Robert grinned from ear to ear.

"I see you're doing what you're <u>second best</u> at, Dale."

"That's right."

As Dale continued to greet the others, Daniel whispered to Father, "What does Robert mean?"

"He means that Dale is always eating, yet he's in great shape. He's the toughest guy I've ever followed up a mountain."

"If he's second best at eating, what's he best at?"

"I expect Rob means deer hunting. He's the best deer hunter I've ever been around."

When Dale got to Daniel, Father introduced him. "Dale, this is my son Daniel. Dan, this is the legendary Dale."

"So this is the young cub. Don't worry about him at all, Dick, I'll take personal charge of him and train him myself..." he leaned closer to Dick and added in a quieter voice, "...before these other guys ruin him." The other hunters groaned and chided Dale about his remark. Dale just stuffed more chips into his mouth and said, "Let's go eat. It smells great up there, but they won't tell me what it is."

He was right. The farther Daniel got up the stairs, the more delicious the aroma became. Ted and Ron also had a nice fire going in the huge rock fireplace. Dale shuffled over to the counter and helped himself to a pickle from a large jar sitting there. It was the biggest pickle Daniel had ever seen.

"Ma Braun made those special for deer camp," Ted remarked. "We all told her how you liked her dill pickles."

Dale let the pickle drop to the carpeted floor. "Stand back everyone. I love her pickles, but I won't eat anything that I can't lift." He assumed a weight lifter's pose and struggled to get the pickle hoisted over his head. The group cheered wildly as he accomplished the task. Dale bowed several times and began chomping on the huge cucumber. "Let's eat, I'm starving."

Everyone found a place at the table. After giving thanks and asking for a safe hunt tomorrow, they all began filling their plates. In the middle of the table was a huge platter of the steaming mystery meat.

Marvin D. Braun

There was also a huge bowl of mixed beans that Spence had made.

"I see Spence that you made your famous bean salad again," Rusty commented.

"Keep those away from me," Todd joked, "Or I'll scare all the deer away tomorrow."

"Whoever guesses what kind of meat this is," Ron remarked, "gets out of doing dishes tonight."

The men began making their guesses. Since Ron was an avid coon hunter, the first guess was raccoon. Other guesses included elk, moose, antelope, deer, squirrel, goose, pheasant, grouse, possum and Robert even suggested porcupine.

"Porcupine!" Todd exclaimed. "What are you trying to do, turn us into pin cushions?" The group laughed.

Suddenly, Dale's leg began jumping uncontrollably. He stood up and hopped over to the kitchen counter, grabbed another pickle from the jar. When he turned around, his front teeth were exposed. He made some clicking noises with his mouth as he took small nibbling bites from the dill. Then, in an Elmer Fudd voice he said, "It's wabbit. Wonny is feeding us wascals wabbit." Everyone let out a cheer as Ron proclaimed Dale the winner.

"No dishes for you tonight Dale."

"Like he ever did any anyway," several in the group jokingly complained.

As all continued to eat, the talk centered around tomorrow's hunting plans.

"I think we need to make a drive on Respirator Ridge," Robert commented.

"Why's it called Respirator Ridge?" Daniel asked.

"If you have to ask, that means you've never climbed up it," Todd answered. "By the time you get to the top, you feel like you should be on a hospital respirator. Respirator Ridge is even steeper than Heart Break Ridge."

"I can't figure you prairie boys out," Dale commented as he chewed on a rabbit bone, "We put you on a small 45% incline that's only about a half mile long with a foot of snow on it, and you guys act like it's difficult. Please pass the rabbit."

The group also talked about what to do in case anyone got lost.

"The first thing you've got to do, is trust your compass," Robert stated. "It's funny how when you're lost, and your sense of direction get's all turned around, that you start distrusting your compass.

Often, what happens is, you're making a drive along a side hill or ridge, and you know that you're supposed to head in a particular direction. Only, the ridges out here usually don't just go in one direction. They twist and turn and, because the trees are so tall and thick that you can't see any landmarks, it's pretty easy to get turned around. The rule is this: Don't cross any fences and don't cross any roads. Most of our drives end on a logging road. When you come to the road, just stop and wait. We'll find you."

"Unless you're Todd," Marlin added. "Then we let you panic for a few hours to see if that Marine training did any good."

"Uh huh, real funny, Marlin," Todd responded. "I was so scared I had to throw away those shorts I was wearing. Had to get a new compass too, darn thing quit working that day." He laughed uproariously at his own joke.

Dick continued the discussion. "Something I've noticed is that occasionally there's another logging road that cuts across the area we're driving. That can be real confusing too, because you're not sure if that's the right road or not."

"Yeah, for all the money we pay you guys for guiding us," Todd joked, "You ought to tell us about those roads."

The truth was, that Robert and Dale were very good guides. They had guided hunters in the Black Hills for many years. Father had told Daniel just how fortunate they were to have such good guides as friends. "Without them, we wouldn't have near the success that we have when we deer hunt up here. These two guys do a lot of scouting for us. They know the areas that we hunt very well. Their preseason work makes things a lot easier and safer for us."

"Don't your topo maps show all those roads?" Robert asked.

"Not nearly all of them," Dick answered, "They just show the main ones."

"What's a topo map?" Daniel asked.

"I was wondering that too," added Todd, "but I was afraid I'd look stupid if I asked!"

"It's way too late for that Todd," Ron quickly kidded. The group laughed again as Todd made one of his goofy faces.

"To answer your question, Daniel," Father replied, "A 'topo' map is a topographical map. It's one of those maps I showed you with all the wiggly lines on it. They show you the elevations as well as the roads, rivers, mountains and stuff."

"All I know is that they're hard to read." Todd spoke again.

"They take some getting used too, but they give you an awful lot of information."

Marlin nodded and continued, "I've learned that the closer the wiggly lines are together, the steeper the hill is going to be."

"Then, after supper, I want to look at Respirator Ridge on your topo map, Todd remarked. "Those little lines should be so close together that it's just solid ink."

The other hunters murmured their agreement. When everyone was absolutely stuffed from the huge meal, Dale spoke, "Just so you know that I won't shirk my duty." He picked up his fork, went into the kitchen and let it drop into the sink. "There, now it's time to teach this young cub how to play potato pool. Come on, Dan." He helped himself to a generous handful of salted peanuts sitting on the counter, "I need to teach you a few things." He winked at Daniel's father and then headed downstairs. As Daniel rose from the table to follow him, Dale's voice could be heard from the basement, "Dan, bring that bowl of peanuts with you when you come downstairs."

Marvin D. Braun

Dale assumed a weight lifter's pose as he prepared to lift the huge pickle.

Chapter 6
Potato Pool

As soon as the table was cleared and the dishes were done, the men began filtering downstairs to join Dale and Daniel playing pool. The discussion turned to the upcoming South Dakota West River Deer Season.

"How's the Tripp County deer hunt looking, Dick?" Marlin asked.

"Good. Daniel and I both got lucky again this year and drew 'any deer' licenses, which means we can shoot a muley or a whitetail."

"Dad and I are going to try something different this year," Daniel continued. "We built a deer blind up on Cupola Hill right above that big batch of plum thickets."

Marlin nodded, "Deer, especially muleys, do seem to like to hole up in those protected pockets once the hunting season starts."

"You've sat up there before, haven't you?" asked Ted.

"Yes, we have," Dick answered. "But when it's cold out, you can only sit so long. By being in our blind and out of the wind, I think we'll be able to sit a lot longer, which increases our chances of seeing a nice buck."

"Another advantage of hunting from a blind as opposed to making a drive," Robert added, "is that you have more time to study a buck's antlers. If you want to shoot a trophy whitetail buck, one that makes the Boone and Crockett Club's record book, the tines have to be at least eight inches long. That means, they have to be approximately as long as the deer's ears. That's hard to tell when a deer is trotting or running through the trees."

"What's Boone and Crockett?" Daniel asked.

"There are two different antler scoring systems. One is called Boone and Crockett and that's a scoring system for deer taken with a firearm. Then there's Pope and Young. That system is for rating racks taken with a bow and arrow."

"Really?" Todd questioned jokingly. "I always thought Pope and Young was for Catholics and Boone and Crockett was for Protestants." He laughed loudly at his joke; the others joined in.

"I think our deer management program is starting to pay off, too," Dick continued.

"What do you mean?" Marlin asked.

"Well, for several years now, Vern, Ralph, and I have agreed not to shoot any buck less than a four-by-four."

"So you've been letting smaller bucks go?"

Marvin D. Braun

"That's right. Last year all four of us took nice deer (see <u>Daniel's First Deer Hunt</u>), but the two previous years, I didn't even pull the trigger. I saw a ton of bucks, but I let them go so they'd have the chance to mature another year.

Daniel and I have done quite a bit of scouting this year and we've seen more big bucks than I can ever remember. You know, everybody likes to shoot big bucks, but, for that to happen, you've got to be willing to let those young bucks go. They need to have a chance to mature. Most bucks get harvested when they're only 1 1/2 to 2 1/2 years old. A deer has to be allowed to reach 4 1/2 or 5 1/2 for them to reach their best. Every year you let a buck go, they get smarter and their chance of surviving to maturity goes way up."

"I agree," Marlin commented, "but our philosophy wasn't always that way. Remember when we used to shoot any deer that we saw just as long as it had horns?"

"I remember. I don't know why we felt we <u>had</u> to shoot a deer just because we had a deer tag. Daniel and I have set a goal for ourselves that we won't shoot a buck this year unless it's bigger than the one we harvested last year. If everyone did that every year, there'd be a lot of trophy bucks around."

"What do you consider a trophy buck?" Spence asked.

"That's different for everybody. If it's your first deer, a doe or a little three point may be a trophy to you..."

Todd interrupted, "Forget about it, Spence. The only trophy buck you're ever gonna get is if you run over one with your pickup." The room erupted in laughter until Dick continued.

"Once you shoot a big buck, it seems pointless to me to harvest a smaller one. I like the idea of trying to get a little nicer buck every year, or at least a buck with a unique rack."

"What do you mean by a unique rack, Dad?" Daniel asked.

"Do you remember that one whitetail buck we saw last year that had the horns that went straight up into the air? They didn't branch at all, but they had a number of little 'sticker' points protruding from the main beam. We let him go last year. It wasn't a huge rack like a six-by-six or anything, but it was very unique. Those kinds of racks are nice to hang on the wall too.

I was talking to Marlo last week and he said he saw that buck. Only now, the rack is even bigger."

"You mean just because his horns were messed up last year, they'll grow the same way this year?"

"Pretty much. Once a buck develops his rack, it stays about the same, except that the antlers get bigger each year until the deer gets really old. Then they start going downhill again."

"Another thing," Marlin added, "Sometimes you may want to eliminate a buck like that from your deer herd because you may not want those genetics passed on. Usually, the size and shape of a buck's antlers are passed on to his offspring. By harvesting that buck, you help to manage the quality of antlers in your herd. On the deer hunting videos, they're actually called 'management' bucks."

"The Black Horned Buck would be a unique buck, wouldn't he?" Daniel asked.

"He sure would be," Marlin answered. "Is he still around, Rob?"

"Dale and I were out scouting two weeks ago and think we saw him."

"It was him all right," Dale cut in. "It was that black-horned, black-eyed, black- hearted devil. He looked just like the Black Stallion. It scared me just to get that close to him." Everyone laughed.

"That's the buck I'd like to get this year." Daniel spoke up.

Dale, who was about to take his next shot, stopped, and laid down his pool stick.

"Son, that's a serious undertaking. I'll tell you what we're going to do." He grabbed the potato they had been playing with from the corner pocket. He placed it carefully near one end of the table. "If you can make this potato, into that pocket, Robert and I will do all we can to help you get that buck." He held his hands up for the group to be quiet. Then in an even louder voice said, "Silence everyone, the boy here is about to become a man."

Marvin D. Braun

Daniel knew it would be a difficult shot. He wasn't that great of a pool player anyway, and the potato wasn't completely round. What a bummer of a thing to decide whether or not he had a chance at the black-horned buck. "Oh, well." he thought to himself, "I might as well give it my best."

He leaned over the table and lined up the cue ball with the potato. Just as he was about to make his shot, Dale startled him by speaking again, "Don't miss…he's a big buck!"

Daniel lined up for the second time… "Black horns," Dale spoke abruptly again, causing everyone in the room to bust out laughing. He walked up behind Daniel and began massaging his shoulders. "I'm rootin' for you all the way, boy. Make that shot." He stepped away and held his hands up for silence again.

Daniel lined up on the potato for the third time. Even Dale was silent this time, as he took his shot…and missed.

The group groaned, except Dale, who quickly picked up the potato and moved it closer to the pocket. "Two out of three," he said.

Daniel took another shot and missed again. "I hope he shoots better than he plays pool." Dale commented as he moved the potato right in front of the pocket and added, "Three out of five, scratches don't count." He had a friendly twinkle in his eye.

Daniel lined up his shot for the fourth time and hit the cue ball as hard as he could. The potato thudded out of sight into the pocket. The room erupted into cheers as Dale picked Daniel up and hoisted him onto his shoulders. "Now I'm going to take this boy upstairs and get him something to eat. He's going to need all of his strength tomorrow spotting and bagging that big, fat, black-horned buck." With that he headed up the stairs.

Chapter 7

Snow

While eating a pickle with Dale, they stepped out onto the deck. It was a beautiful night, and you hardly needed a coat.

Daniel's father, Marlin, Robert and Spence joined them on the deck. In the distance they could hear coyotes howling.

"It'll be different by morning," Dale commented. "It's supposed to snow tonight, which should make for some great deer hunting tomorrow."

"Why does snow help?" Daniel asked.

Marlin answered, "The main reason, is because you can see the deer better. Also, because you can see their fresh tracks, you can tell which trails they're using. It helps to set up an ambush."

"For whitetails at least," Robert added. "Whitetails tend to travel on established trails a lot more than muleys do, or, at least they do until they get spooked."

"Where do you think we're going to start tomorrow morning?" Marlin asked.

"Why don't we go after the Black-Horned Buck?" Daniel questioned anxiously.

Pickle juice sprayed into Daniel's face as Dale put his arm around Daniel's shoulders and answered the question.

"Dan, have you ever seen what a pickle looks like after it's puked up on a rock?" Daniel nodded his head no and Dale continued. "I didn't think so. Well, you don't want to, 'cause it ain't pretty. Now look over that way." He pointed to a very large hill silhouetted by the moonlight, "Do you see that hill?" This time Daniel nodded yes. "That monster is Big Black Buck Ridge.

Do you feel like climbing that long, steep, heartbreaking, leg-killing hill first thing in the morning, especially after eating all these pickles?" Daniel grinned as he shook his head no. "Well, that's where that big black-horned buck likes to hide out, so we'll save that hunt until later. I say we start with the 385 Strip. It's close, so we don't have to get up as early."

Everyone agreed that sounded like a good plan. They visited on the deck for a while longer, and as they did, the sky started clouding up and the air got noticeably colder.

"You can almost smell the snow," Spence commented, breathing in a huge lung full of air.

Daniel sniffed the air. It still smelled wonderfully like pine trees, but in the last few minutes, the air had taken on a different aroma. It was hard to describe it, except that it smelled like snow!

Todd poked his head out the door, "I'm supposed to ask if any of you little girls want to play a game of pitch?"

Pitch was the family card game. Whenever relatives got together, they often played a game or two of pitch. Daniel had learned how to play several years ago. All the men on the deck enthusiastically agreed and moved inside. The group played for an hour and then Daniel's father looked at his watch.

"Five o'clock's going to get here mighty early in the morning; I'm going to bed." The others agreed and began shuffling off to bed.

Dale stepped out the door and onto the balcony. "Come and look," he called from outside. They all moved outside and onto the deck. Huge snowflakes were floating down from the sky. He added, "If this keeps up for very long, it'll be totally white by morning, and then," he put his arm around Daniel's shoulders again, "we'll just have to see how smart Mr. Black-Horned Buck will be." He stepped behind Daniel and began massaging his shoulders like a coach does to his boxer. "This boy can shoot straight, can't he, Dick?"

Dick chuckled as he answered. "Dan's a good shot, he's practiced quite a bit with his new rifle."

"Good, then I guess you're ready. Do you need another pickle?" Daniel laughed and nodded his head no. "Okay, then you better get some sleep."

The group observed the snow for a few minutes and then everyone went to bed.

Daniel was so excited about tomorrow's hunt, that he had trouble getting to sleep. He kept thinking about the Black-Horned Buck. He was in a deep sleep when Father gently woke him at five o'clock A.M. Daniel could smell the aroma of freshly brewed coffee, so Father must have been awake for awhile already.

"Look outside, Daniel," Father encouraged. Daniel got up and peered out the window. The ground was totally white and the snow was still filtering down. Even the branches of the pine trees had a couple inches of snow on them.

Robert came trudging up the basement steps. "Where's my hunting knife? I'm going to have to perform some surgery on Ted and Ronny."

"I take it the boys must have snored a little during the night," Marlin chuckled.

"Only enough to scare away all the deer and keep me from getting any sleep. I figure if I carve out their tonsils and uvulas, that'll help."

Dale moved into the living room. "Won't help," he said, "I tried that last year." Everyone laughed and then looked outside as they saw headlights turn into the driveway.

"Clyde's here," Ken called from the basement. They all watched as the suburban made it half-way up the steep driveway, then had to back down and try again. On the third try he made it, but only after putting the vehicle into four-wheel drive. The group, now out on the deck watching, cheered as Clyde successfully pulled up to the front door.

"Morning, Clyde, morning Lee," Marlin greeted the two brothers as they stepped out of the suburban. Each had a cup of coffee in their hands. "Come on up, we've got a fresh pot of coffee brewing."

Marvin D. Braun

Suddenly, Todd stepped out from under the balcony and into view. All he was wearing was his blaze orange cap, hunting boots and undershorts.

"You guys ready, yet?" He called to the group up above, "Clyde and Lee are ready to go." Then walking to Clyde and Lee he whispered loudly, "I tried to get them to go to bed early last night, but they just wouldn't listen." He laughed uproariously at his own joke then added, "Brrrr…it's chilly out here. Does anybody else feel a breeze?" He moved quickly indoors to get dressed, still laughing.

Ron's voice could be heard from the basement, "How's a guy supposed to get any sleep around here with all the racket? Morning Lee, morning Clyde. You guys hungry? I'll fix you some eggs."

Lee responded, "I was hungry until I saw Todd in his underwear!"

The group drank coffee and visited as everyone finished getting dressed for the morning's hunt.

"I hope you got some different boots from last year, Ken," Marlin commented. "It's going to be pretty slick out there this morning."

"Yeah, I did. Last year was enough for me. I must have fallen a dozen times last year because of those stupid boots. They were new, too."

"Yes, but the soles were made of that hard plastic. When it gets cold and slick, those things are worthless walking on these side hills. The absolute best hunting boots are the kind that have those little rubber air-bobs on the sole. Even if you step on a wet or icy rock, they've got good traction."

Daniel remembered his father telling him about Ken's experience. "Ken came limping out of the woods like he'd been beaten up. He was bloody and limping and had even chipped the butt of his rifle on a rock, he had fallen so hard."

After that, Father had ordered Daniel a new set of hunting boots with the air-bob soles.

When everyone was ready, Robert and Dale gave the final instructions for the hunt they were about to make. Daniel was to be one of the blockers along with Lee, Clyde and Marlin. Daniel's father, Ken, Robert, and Dale would be the walkers. Spence, who was still sleeping, and Ted and Ron, were planning on

Marvin D. Braun

going to the old western town of Deadwood for sight seeing.

As the eight hunters got into the appropriate vehicle, Ted and Ron wished them good luck and waved good bye to them from the balcony. Then, grinning, they each grabbed a handful of snow to go wake up Spence.

Chapter 8

The Strip

The hunters had named this hunt the 385 Strip because they made their drive along a half-mile wide strip of land that bordered Highway 385 between Hill City and Deadwood.

It was just light enough to shoot when they dropped off Dale, Robert, Ken, Todd, and Dick at the junction of Highway 385 and a logging road that entered the forest 1/2 mile south of the cabin. Then, Daniel and Marlin drove Robert's pickup one mile farther to the

Marvin D. Braun

next logging road. Lee and Clyde followed them in Clyde's suburban.

They all got out of their vehicles quietly and whispered among themselves briefly before beginning their walk up the mountain. After traveling several hundred yards, Lee, who was the oldest of the group, dropped off. The remaining three moved slowly up the hill.

It was hard to be quiet because the ground was very treacherous. You couldn't see what was underfoot as the rocks, branches and roots that littered the ground were covered with six inches of snow. Several times, Daniel nearly tripped when he looked back to see if he could spot Lee and his foot hooked on a hidden stick.

The incline was very steep, which made the going even tougher. He was puffing loudly by the time Marlin and Clyde decided to stop for a breather. It was impressive how physically fit Marlin, Clyde, and Lee were. He hoped he would be that physically fit when he was that old.

Daniel and the Black Horned Buck

Marlin and Clyde whispered to each other and Daniel could see Clyde pointing toward an old, dead, uprooted tree. He guessed that's where Clyde would be waiting. Daniel glanced back down the hill towards Lee, but could no longer see him because of the pine trees and underbrush.

Clyde grinned at him and whispered, "Good luck, young 'un." Then he moved carefully toward the uprooted tree. As Daniel and Marlin began moving upward again, Daniel looked back and saw Clyde brushing the wet snow from the stump. "Good idea," thought Daniel. "That way, your butt wouldn't get all wet when the snow melted."

The two of them climbed for several minutes more until they reached a treeless, flat, plateau. At one end of the small clearing was a large pile of rocks. Marlin pointed to the rocks and said quietly, "That's a great place to sit. I've taken two bucks myself from this spot. Look at that trail over there; it looks like a deer highway. Find a comfortable spot to sit in those rocks and just wait. It'll probably take 'em forty-five minutes to an hour to get here. Dale or Robert should come

Marvin D. Braun

through this way. I'm going to go a little farther." He started walking, stopped, and came back, "Remember, you can only shoot a buck, and, to be legal, the buck has to have at least two points on one side." He gave Daniel a smile and a thumbs up, and then headed across the clearing and out of sight.

Daniel picked out a flat rock, wiped the snow off of it, and then sat down. He wasn't very happy with his field of fire, so he picked out another rock that was a little higher up. Satisfied that he could see the entire clearing, he wiped the snow off of it and sat down.

Checking his watch, he was surprised that it was only 6:30 A.M. He zipped up his coat. It wasn't that cold out, but he had sweat quite a bit on the hard climb up the steep slope. Back home, the time was 7:30 and he would have already been getting ready for school. He smiled to himself, deer hunting beat going to school any day, even if it was hard work.

Although, this was only Daniel's second deer season, he knew that a successful deer hunt depended on a *lot* of preparation, and a *little* luck.

Daniel and the Black Horned Buck

They were very lucky to have Robert and Dale guide them to such good deer hunting spots.

Daniel settled down to wait. Uncle Marlin told him it would take the walkers forty-five minutes or more to make the mile long hike. Of course, deer could venture by anytime, so it was best to be as still, and as quiet, as possible to have the greatest chance at bagging a buck, especially the big black-horned buck.

His mind drifted as he waited, thinking of last summer when his family had gone camping in the Black Hills. Father had driven into Rapid City to get groceries. Mother had stayed at the tent to start getting supper ready and his sister Angie, Dougy, and himself had gone swimming in the campground's pool. A very sudden storm came up and it started hailing. The hailstones were as big as tennis balls, so he, Angie, and Dougy had quickly gone inside a small tin shed next to the pool for shelter. Later, he told his parents that they knew Dougy was crying, but even though his mouth was wide open, neither he nor Angie could hear him crying, because the hail was so loud on the metal roof.

The hail had actually punched holes right through the tent roof. Poor Mother, after quickly looking to see that her children were safe inside the tin shed, she had huddled in the tent with a pillow over her head to protect herself.

The family certainly hadn't had good luck camping. The summer before, they had gone camping with Uncle Marlin, Spence, Ken, and their families in North Dakota. A wind storm came up their very first night there and destroyed their tent. Two wrecked tents in two years was enough for Daniel's parents. They hadn't been camping since.

Suddenly, Daniel sensed he was not alone. He wasn't even sure why. He hadn't actually heard or seen anything. He moved his eyes, not his head, to see if he could detect what had aroused him. Out of the corner of one eye, he saw a flicker of movement as an ear twitched nervously. It was a buck, the hugest buck Daniel had ever seen. The critter was only about thirty yards away and partly shielded by trees.

Daniel and the Black Horned Buck

Daniel's heart raced as he carefully brought his rifle to his shoulder. The buck's antlers filled his scope as he began taking aim. He flipped his rifle's safety to the off position, and took aim. He settled the cross hairs of the scope on the animal's mid section, just behind the shoulders. He began to squeeze the trigger and then stopped. Something just didn't seem right. The buck was too big...the antlers were different...and it had a mane. It was an elk! Daniel eased his rifle off his shoulder and put the safety back on.

Whew! That was close. He was very glad that Father had warned him about elk and explained the difference between deer and elk. He also remembered what Mr. Ludkey, their game warden, had told them many times in the hunter's safety course: "Always think twice **before** you pull the trigger."

The bull elk was looking away from Daniel, towards its back trail. When done, it sniffed the air carefully before walking across the clearing. Daniel was glad the light breeze was blowing his scent away from the elk. The huge five-by-five apparently hadn't smelled him, and passed within twenty yards before disappearing into the forest on the other side of the clearing.

Wow! The guys were never going to believe this. He wanted to jump up and go look at the elk's tracks immediately, but figured he'd better stay put, in case a deer came by. One thing was for sure, once you were that close to an elk, you wouldn't forget what one looked like again.

He heard some rustling across the clearing. A doe and a fawn nervously trotted out of the woods. By the way they acted, Daniel could tell that they had been spooked. More than likely, it was by the hunters walking this way. Suddenly, another small deer entered the clearing. After studying it closely, Daniel could see small spikes protruding from its head. It was a buck, but not big enough to be legal.

KABOOM! The shot rang out from Daniel's left, in the direction that Marlin had gone. Daniel gripped his rifle tightly, ready, in case a wounded deer, or any decent buck came into view. At the sound of Marlin's shot, the spike buck raced off in the direction it had come.

Daniel waited for ten more minutes, and was wondering what to do, when a whistle startled him. He saw Dale's colorful blaze-orange camo coat coming toward him through the trees.

"Did you get one, Dan?"

"It wasn't me, but it might have been Marlin."

"Well, somebody sure did. That bullet hit meat, I heard it go thwack. Let's go check." Did you see anything?"

Daniel told him about the elk.

Dale smiled and said, "They're huge, aren't they? I saw elk tracks and fresh elk droppings in several spots this morning. I figured we might chase an elk by somebody. I was just hoping nobody would shoot one."

As they walked in the direction of the shot, the terrain changed so that they were walking on a very steep side hill. Daniel was carrying his rifle on his right shoulder by its sling. He was having trouble keeping his balance. His feet kept slipping downhill on the wet snow.

"Stop," Dale said. "Let me show you something that might save your rifle and a broken bone or two. I had to explain this to your Uncle Marlin when he first started hunting out here, but not before he banged up his scope so bad on a rock that he missed the next two bucks that he shot at.

When you walk on a side hill, whether you carry your rifle in your hand or by its sling, carry it on the downhill side. That way, if you fall, and you always tend to fall into the side of the hill, at least you have a free hand to catch yourself with. It saves your rifle and it's safer, too."

"Thanks Dale." Daniel tried Dale's suggestion. It worked much better on the slick side hill.

"There's Marly." Dale pointed through the trees. "Looks like he got himself a buck."

As they approached closer, Daniel could see Marlin, his jacket hanging on a nearby branch, his sleeves rolled up, and a knife in his hand working on a deer.

"Nice little four by four whitetail, Marlin." Dale commented. Daniel was surprised by how small the buck's antlers were. There were four points on each side, but they were much shorter and smaller than the bucks that most of the guys shot back home. The deer's body was also considerably smaller.

As if reading his mind, Marlin spoke, "Nothing like one of those corn-fed monster bucks you guys raise back in Gregory County, but I guess he'll do for a Black Hills buck."

They helped Marlin finish field-dressing his deer, then tied a chunk of rope to his horns, and began dragging it back toward the vehicles. The first fifty yards were extremely difficult, because they had to pull the buck up the slick side hill. It seemed like every two feet they pulled it uphill, it slid one foot back downhill. Once they got to the top, it became much easier. Then, they almost had to hold the deer from sliding down the hill too fast. The only problem was, its legs and antlers kept getting tangled in small trees, rocks and dead logs.

"You have to be careful," Dale cautioned. "I heard about a guy who was doing this, and the deer slid into the back of his legs, and he fell backwards onto the deer's antlers. It sounds stupid, but the guy was by himself, and it cut an artery in his leg and he almost bled to death."

Marlin continued, "I never think it's a good idea to hunt alone. No matter how careful you are, accidents can still happen. At least, if you have a hunting partner, you have someone checking on you."

They took turns pulling the deer and carrying each other's rifles. They had unloaded all of the rifles before they started back toward the vehicles.

"One thing that always bothered me," Dale remarked, "was when you were walking down a hill and the hunter just ahead of you on the trail still had a bullet in the chamber of his rifle. Did you ever notice how often that muzzle is pointed right at your head? I just don't allow it anymore. The instant you're done with a drive or coming out of your stand, you unload." Marlin and Daniel agreed.

Daniel and the Black Horned Buck

"Hey, Dale, do you want to help me play a little joke on Todd?" Marlin asked.

"Sure, what do I need to do?"

"I saw a guy do this to one of his buddies in Montana." Marlin reached into his pocket and pulled out a little plastic baggy with eleven or twelve brown M & M's in it. "They look amazingly like elk droppings, don't they? I'll just drop them in the snow right next to those elk tracks we saw by the suburban. Just follow my lead."

Dale grinned. He had a mischievous look on his face as he agreed.

By the time they got the rest of the way down the hill, all of the others were standing around the trucks visiting. They questioned each other about who had seen what, and how Marlin had got his deer. When he had a chance, Daniel told the group about the five-by-five bull elk. Out of the corner of his eye, he noticed Marlin kneel down beside the trail and drop the M & M's in the snow.

"Speaking of elk, here's some tracks right here, and some droppings," Marlin commented.

"I saw a bunch of tracks, too," Dale joined in. He walked over to Marlin and knelt beside him. He picked up one of the M & M's and examined it closely. "How old would you say this is Marly, two or three hours?" His tone was very serious.

Marlin also picked up one of the candies, studied it carefully, sniffed it, then placed it in his mouth and began chewing on it before he answered. "I don't know, might be a tad longer than that, maybe even four or five hours."

Todd had been watching the two hunters, and knew that both of them had hunted elk a lot. "Are you nuts?" he asked incredulously as Dale also began chewing on one of the M & M's. "I'd say you both have been in the hills way too long!" He shook his head disbelievingly.

Marlin spoke. "Anybody else want to try one? They sure taste a lot like M & M's."

Chapter 9
Arrow Heads

The group laughed for several minutes about the joke Marlin and Dale had played on Todd. The nice thing about Todd, and one of the things that made him so likable, was that he could laugh at himself.

"Where do we go next, Robert? Marlin asked.

"Dick or Clyde, you guys got any ideas?"

Dale spoke up, "Let's leave Respirator Ridge until later. Right now that Black-Horned Buck is still probably wide awake. If we wait until this afternoon, maybe we can catch him sleeping."

"How about the Palmer Gulch drive?" Dick suggested. "That's one of my favorite spots in the Black Hills."

"You just like it, because on that drive, we don't have to walk any hills," joked Dale.

"Sounds good to me. Are there any elk there? I'm getting hungry," commented Todd, laughing again at his own joke.

"I'm not sure Clyde wants to go there," Marlin said. "Remember, that's where he tangled with that bullet-proof buck." Clyde groaned.

"Now why did you have to go and bring that up again? You guys don't need to worry," Clyde spoke up. "I got myself some different bullets." He held up a cartridge. "These babies are magnums." Everyone chuckled.

Daniel remembered Father telling him the story. Several years ago, the group made the Palmer Gulch drive. Clyde was blocking, and according to him, this nice four-point buck trotted out of the trees and stood broadside to him at only fifty yards. Clyde claimed he shot and hit the buck four times, but the bullets were defective, so they just bounced off his skin.

The group had kidded him about it ever since. The Christmas after the hunt, they had each sent him a box of bullets.

Everyone climbed into the vehicles and they drove toward Palmer Gulch.

"Didn't Palmer Gulch used to be an old Indian hideout?" Ken asked.

Marlin answered, "After the Battle of the Little Big Horn, Crazy Horse and a band of his Lakota warriors hid out around here somewhere. I'm not sure it was Palmer Gulch, though. If not, it was right in this area."

As they passed the Palmer Gulch Campground, Father pointed to the south. "That's Harney Peak, Daniel. It's the highest point in the Black Hills. Some day I'd like to take you and the rest of the family on a hike up to there."

"Do you start from here, Dad? That looks awfully long and steep. Dougy would be complaining about his legs being tired before we got one block."

Father chuckled. "No, you start from Sylvan Lake. There's a hiking trail that goes all the way up there, one that I think even your brother Douglas could handle. Sylvan Lake is a nice place to trout fish, too."

"Do you fish for trout different than bass?"

"There are several ways to fish for trout. One way, is to fish during the daytime and use artificial lures just like the ones we use for bass. I've had pretty good luck with Mepp's Spinners. Another way, is fishing at night from a boat. You just drop your line clear to the bottom. It's pretty similar to walleye fishing. We always baited our hooks with kernels of canned corn."

Todd commented from the front seat, "That way Daniel, when you get hungry, you just take a bite of corn." The carload of hunters groaned.

Father continued, "The third way, is by fly-fishing. I've never fished that way, but it's something I'd like to learn how to do. Bob fishes that way all the time."

"What's fly-fishing like?" Daniel asked.

"It takes some special fishing tackle," Father answered. "You need a fly-rod-and-reel."

Todd quickly spoke up, "I did that once, and I know why they call it a fly-rod. After I didn't catch anything and got tangled up in the line for about the tenth time, that rod flew through the air really good." He hooted loudly at his comment.

"It does take a special knack," chuckled Father, "because the artificial flies that you use as bait are so light, you can't cast them out with a regular rod-and-reel. A fly-rod has very light line, you use it kind of like a whip."

"Well, here we are," Clyde announced, as he pulled off the highway and onto a logging trail. Robert and Dale had stopped just ahead of them. They got out of the pickup and came back to the suburban.

"Marlin, you, Dick and Daniel come with Dale and me. Clyde, we're going to give you a chance to redeem yourself. You string the blockers out along this road."

"I'm scared, Robert," Todd complained jokingly. "What if that mean four-point comes at me?"

"Give me your bullet, Todd." Dale ordered. Todd handed Dale a cartridge. Dale examined it carefully.

Then he tossed it into the air a couple of times, rubbed it under each arm pit, spit on it, and handed it back to Todd. "You should be okay now, buddy. But, remember, you've only got one shot, so wait until you can see the whites of his eyes."

Clyde groaned, "All right you wise guys, let's get going."

Marlin, Father and Daniel got out of Clyde's suburban and climbed into the back of Robert's pickup.

As they were driving down the road to the next trail where they were going to begin the drive, Father said, "This is one of the prettiest hunts we go on. This area is loaded with small pine trees. They're so thick, you can't see but a few feet ahead of you. Then, every so often, there's huge rock formations. It's an awesome walk, about a mile long. Just take it nice and easy."

Robert turned the pickup into a rough, narrow trail, then stopped. "Dan, why don't you get out first. Give the rest of us about ten minutes to get into position, then just start walking nice and slow. Your compass heading should be straight east." Daniel nodded in agreement, and Robert drove off. He checked the time and watched as they drove two-hundred yards down the road and let out Father. The pickup disappeared around the corner of the trail before he could see who got out next.

The ten minutes passed slowly. Finally, he saw Father wave and start moving slowly into the trees. Daniel loaded a bullet into the chamber of his rifle and made sure the safety was on before moving into the woods himself. Every few minutes, he looked in the direction of his father. Usually, he couldn't see him, but occasionally, if the trees thinned a little bit, he could catch a glimpse of Father's blaze- orange coat or hat.

Father had explained to him how important it was to try and stay even with the other walkers when making a hunting drive. "You should try to all walk the same speed, whether you're deer hunting or pheasant hunting. You need to continually be checking and rechecking your position. Getting too far ahead or behind is dangerous. Imagine if you were a hundred yards behind the other hunters, and a deer suddenly jumped up in front and to the side of you. You can't see any of the other hunters because the forest is too thick, so you could be shooting right at one of them."

"Then how do you know how fast to walk if you can't see the other walkers?" Daniel had asked.

"It comes with experience, and familiarity with your companion's hunting style. But, most of all, just pay attention. Usually, you can catch at least an occasional glimpse of the guy next to you. Hopefully, he's doing the same thing. You know, Dan, I've actually refused to to hunt with certain people because I didn't approve of their hunting methods or tactics. If someone is careless when handling a gun, I refuse to hunt with them."

The pine trees thickened and as Daniel brushed against the lower branches of one, the snow that was piled on the upper branches, cascaded down on top of him. Some of it even went down the back of his neck. It was very cold.

He had been carrying his rifle slung over his right shoulder, so he quickly took it down and checked the scope. Sure enough, the snow had landed on the front lens, and if not cleaned off, would have blocked his vision with his scope.

He smiled to himself. This was only his second deer hunting season, and already he was a smarter hunter. Last year, the same thing had happened. Only, he didn't know it until he spotted a deer. As he had tried to take aim, he realized that his scope was blocked with snow. That mistake had prevented him from bagging the nicest muley buck on Uncle Ted's ranch last year.

He shivered from the cold snow down his neck, and started moving forward again. The trees thinned and were replaced by a huge block of granite nearly the size of a house. By the tracks in the snow, Daniel was amazed to see that some deer had actually climbed on top of the giant rock. He decided to follow the tracks, and had a difficult time getting where the deer had gone.

He reached the top, and was wondering why any deer could, or would, climb on top of such a big rock, when a shot rang out ahead of him and to his left. It sounded muffled through the snow covered trees. He quickly decided that standing twenty feet in the air, on top of a boulder, with bullets flying through the air, wasn't a very good idea. As he began climbing down, he nearly slipped on the wet boulder. Thank goodness, the air-bob soles had caught just in time.

He continued moving slowly forward, but never did see Father, or any deer; the pine trees were just too thick. He was beginning to wonder if he was lost, when he spotted some blaze-orange up ahead. It was Todd.

"Did you see anything?" Daniel asked.

Todd nodded. "Yes, I did. I had a little three-point mess around in front of me for a couple of minutes. He was legal, but I'd rather wait for something bigger. He'll be a lot nicer next year."

They moved out of the trees and began walking down the trail toward the other hunters.

"Sounds like somebody might have got one down here," Todd commented. "There's Lee and your dad."

They joined them and continued visiting as they moved down the road. The snow was crisscrossed by deer tracks.

Daniel and the Black Horned Buck

As they progressed a little farther, Marlin came limping out of the woods.

"Oooo, I think I just about broke my butt bone. I climbed up on this big rock and slipped coming down."

Daniel chuckled. "Me too, Uncle Marlin. I guess air-bobs don't stick to everything."

Soon they came upon the rest of the group. Clyde was just finishing tagging a decent three-by-four buck.

"I see the new bullets worked," Robert commented.

"Yup, he never knew what hit him," Clyde answered.

The hunters visited about the hunt as Lee took Robert around to get his pickup.

"Marlin thinks we need to change the name of this hunt to Busted Butt Drive," Todd offered. Everyone else began suggesting different names until Ken, who had been kicking around under the snow exclaimed, "Well what have we got here?" He held up an Indian arrow head.

"Where did you find that?" Marlin asked.

"I was just telling everybody that this area used to be an old Indian hideout," Ken answered. "I thought

Marvin D. Braun

I'd just kick around a little bit, and I found this arrow head."

The group was examining the arrowhead when Todd exclaimed, "Here's another one!" He proudly held up his find.

Everyone quickly started kicking the snow off the road, searching for more arrow heads. Dale was on his hands and knees scraping the snow off the ground. Within five minutes, they had found four more and were still searching, when Marlin questioned, "Wait a minute, these look a little too shiny to be here for over one hundred years. What's going on?"

Ken and Todd busted out laughing. "They sure do," Ken replied. "They also look a lot like those arrow heads you can buy at Wall Drug."

"I guess, you could call that getting even," Todd continued. He had been in on the joke with Ken.

Suddenly, Dale held up his hands for silence, "Shhhh, listen."

The sun had come out and the weather had warmed up considerably since they had started hunting earlier this morning. The snow that had collected on the branches of the pine trees was starting to melt. As it did, it slid off, fell to the ground, and made a 'plopping' sound. All around them now in the forest, there was a continual sound of, "Plop, plop, plop."

"Let's get going," Dale said. "This snow dropping off the trees covers up most of the noise you make as a hunter, and the constant motion of the snow falling off the branches makes your movement less noticeable. It's the best chance we're ever going to get at bagging the Black-Horned Buck. Let's head for Respirator Ridge."

No one argued as they climbed into the vehicles.

Chapter 10
Respirator Ridge

"The boy comes with me; also Todd, Marlin, and Ken." Dale gave the orders. "Robert, you line the blockers up at the bottom."

Robert and Lee had returned with the vehicles. The blockers got into Clyde's suburban, and the walkers into Robert's pickup.

When on their way, Todd commented, "Wow, Dan, how did you get so lucky to be picked as one of the

Daniel and the Black Horned Buck

walkers on this drive? Now you get to find out what climbing Respirator Ridge is like."

"I guess you only get one chance in a lifetime to actually block while sitting on Big Black Buck Rock," Ken joked. "I got a buck there three years ago, and Dale has made me walk ever since. I don't really think it's right that I should get punished just because I'm the only one that can shoot straight."

"Shoot straight?" Dale questioned. "As I recall, the deer ran so close to you that you didn't even use your scope. You just pulled the trigger as he ran by you on the trail." Todd, Daniel and Marlin hooted at the story.

"You sure make it sound less exciting than it was," Ken continued, acting like his feelings were hurt. "It was pretty darn scary sitting on that rock all by myself."

"I have a serious question for you, Dale," Marlin spoke. "If you really want Daniel to get the Black Horned Buck, why is he walking? Wouldn't he have a better chance sitting and blocking on Big Black Buck Rock?"

"Normally, I would say yes," Dale responded. "But with the way the snow is falling off the trees, I've just got a hunch that his best chance today is by walking right down the middle of this drive, through those real thick, heavy trees."

The logging road they were traveling on was very rough and Dale was driving fast. As they hit a hole, Daniel bounced so high that his head hit the top of the cab of the pickup. All the passengers let out a loud shout.

"Dale," Todd pointed, "over there. You don't want to miss that hole, do you?"

Marlin added, "If you don't slow down, you're going to kill the boy before he gets a chance at bagging that buck."

Dale grinned. "You sissies better quit complaining. This is what we call Hill's Four-Wheeling. Get it out of your systems, I don't want you to make any noise going up Respirator."

"Oh, like that's going to happen," Marlin replied. "I'll be able to hear Todd's heart beating in his chest at a hundred yards."

Dale continued to drive. They took several turnoffs and the road was so windy that Daniel had no idea which direction they were going. Finally, Dale pulled the pickup off the trail and right up to a small creek. He pointed straight ahead. "There it is, Daniel. That's the infamous Respirator Ridge."

Daniel gazed ahead at the tree-covered slope. He couldn't even see the top of the ridge through the pickup windshield.

"Oh, it's a beaut, Dan. You're going to love it." Todd slapped him on the back and guffawed. "Especially trying to keep up with Dale."

Marlin agreed. "Every year I run and lift weights just so I can keep up with Dale and Robert. Never seems to be enough, though."

"Dad told me that he climbed the Gregory buttes at least 1800 times this past year, just to stay in shape for this hunt," Daniel told the others.

"No kidding," Dale commented. "That's impressive. If I'd have known that, I'd have his butt over here walking with us."

They all chuckled, then began silently getting out of the pickup and getting their gear ready. Dale suggested that they not put a bullet in the chamber of their rifles until they reached the top. He also recommended that they shed a layer or two of clothing. "I don't think you'll have any trouble staying warm on this one, boys." He had a twinkle in his eye. "Just make sure you still have some blaze orange showing."

"Dale, I have a suggestion," Todd offered quietly. "Why don't you drag a rope to the top, then maybe you could pull us up."

Dale walked over to Todd and put his arm around him, "Todd, I wouldn't want you to miss this climb for anything in the world." Then, more seriously, he added, "Listen, guys, I really think we've got a good chance at bagging a buck or two on this drive; maybe even the Black Horned Buck. The weather conditions are in our favor. Let's go. We'll take it nice and easy."

Dale led them down to the creek, where they all had to jump across. Then they began their ascent. By the time Dale stopped the first time, all except Dale were puffing loudly. When Todd caught his breath enough so he could talk, he commented, "Dale, your idea of nice and easy must be different than mine." He chuckled quietly.

The higher they climbed, the steeper the ridge became. They had to stop three or four times before they finally reached the summit. Daniel had to admit it was one of the hardest workouts he'd ever had.

Dale let them rest for a couple of minutes before he began giving them their final instructions.

"Okay, boys, the hard part is over. From here on, it's downhill all the way."

"Good thing," Todd gasped, "I could start to feel the plaque flowing in my arteries." Everyone laughed quietly.

Dale continued, "Let me show you something." He led them to the other side of the summit to an opening in the trees. "Welcome to paradise, gentlemen," he exclaimed. "That is Big Black Buck Draw and down there, about three-fourths of a mile, is Big Black Buck Rock."

It was one of the most awesome sights Daniel had ever seen. The forest dropped off over the top of the ridge like a beautiful hidden valley. With the sun shining on the bright snow, the sight was dazzling. In the distance, on the left side of the basin, Daniel could see a huge, rock-covered mound sticking up through the trees.

Dale pointed to it. "Ken, you take the left side of the mound. Marlin, you've done the mound before. I want you to go right up over the top. It's going to be very treacherous because of the snow."

"Dan, I want you to be between Marly and Todd, so keep the mound on your left. Marlin is going to be right up on top of that monster. You are going to go through some timber that is thicker than hair on a dog's back. Take it slow, bucks like to hide in that thick stuff."

"Todd, you and I are gonna go to the right a hundred yards. You're going to take the opposite side of the valley. It'll be tough keeping your sense of direction in those tall trees, but just do the best you can following that side hill down to the bottom. I'm going to follow the very top of the ridge down."

"Whatever you do, don't wander over the top of this right-hand ridge. I don't know where we'd find you if you did that. There isn't even a road for about three miles. Dan and Todd, you give the rest of us about ten minutes to get into positions. Any questions?"

All shook their heads no. "Okay then, good luck." Then he turned to Daniel, "Dan, I hope you get him." Daniel hoped so too.

Chapter 11
Old Blackie

Daniel checked his watch several times as he waited for the others to get into position. The snow was falling off the branches continually now, making the forest just a blur of sound and movement.

When the ten minutes were past, he loaded a shell into the chamber of his rifle and put the safety on. Then he began moving forward slowly into Big Black Buck Draw. Even though it was down hill, it was still difficult walking because the melting snow made the rocks and logs slippery.

Almost immediately, he encountered pine trees so thick that he couldn't get through them. He moved to his left until he came upon a trail in the snow that lead through a small opening in the trees. He studied the tracks and noticed that several of the hoof prints were quite large. His heart beat a little faster wondering if they had been made by the black-horned buck.

He followed the trail as it meandered crookedly through the passageways in the trees. Deer were pretty smart, generally, if you wanted the easiest route through the woods, all you had to do was follow their natural trails. Their paths might not be the straightest or the shortest, but they usually were the easiest.

As he moved lower into the draw, the makeup of the trees began to change. The top of the hill had been entirely pine trees. Now, he began seeing aspen, birch and even an occasional oak tree. Daniel smiled to himself. So, that's why the black-horned buck liked to hang out in this spot; he liked eating the acorns from the oak trees.

He stopped every so often to look, listen, and check his compass. Several melted spots in the snow showed where three deer had bedded down. He moved carefully forward to the edge of a small clearing and froze when he spotted them, a doe and her two half-grown fawns moving slowly on the same path he was on. Every time a large chunk of snow plopped to the ground, the doe's ears would flicker nervously, and her body would tense suspiciously. Deer always seemed nervous, but with the snow dropping off the trees like it was, it must be particularly hard on their nerve systems. It reminded Daniel of their cat when he and Dougy would tease her. Whenever her tail would twitch back and forth, they knew she would be ready to go into the attack mode. Daniel was glad that deer were afraid of people. Imagine if they would attack you like Dougy's cat, especially a buck with antlers.

He didn't want to spook the three deer, so he waited patiently while they fidgeted around in the clearing, pawing through the snow looking for grass and acorns. Suddenly, Daniel had an unusual feeling.

Daniel and the Black Horned Buck

The hairs on the back of his neck stood up. He remembered having the same feeling once before when hunting coyotes with his father. Father had been blowing the coyote call, which sounded like a rabbit in distress, when Daniel felt the hair on the back of his neck bristle. He turned to look behind him, and there had been a coyote only ten feet away. Daniel laughed about it now, but it had been pretty scary. The coyote must have been just as scared, because the instant he recognized that Daniel wasn't a rabbit, he went from zero to sixty in about two seconds.

Daniel had that same feeling now, he felt like he was being watched. He moved only his eyes, searching the forest for whatever it was that was causing him to feel the way he did. He saw nothing, so slowly, he turned his head as far as he could to his right. All he could see were trees, until a slight glint of sunlight off an antler made him spot the buck.

He was nearly impossible to see, and Daniel would have missed him completely, except for the sensation that he was being watched. The buck was only about thirty yards away, and Daniel could barely make out his face peering at him through the heavy brush. The animal was apparently bedded down behind a large, brushy log. He slowly brought his rifle up to his shoulder and peered through his scope. It was difficult finding the buck situated where he was in the thick underbrush. Everything looked out of focus in his scope.

His fingers nervously felt for the adjustment knob to turn his scope down to a lower power. With the buck this close, he would be able to see him more clearly with his scope set at a lower power. Suddenly, the deer came into focus, and for a brief instant, Daniel could see the beautiful set of black antlers. It was the black-horned buck!

As carefully as he could, Daniel slipped off his glove and his thumb snapped off the safety. He felt as if his heart would pound through his chest. He peered through his scope again, this time ready to make the shot.

He was sure he was looking in the same spot, but he couldn't locate the buck. He studied the log carefully, but could see nothing of the deer. Then, one of the branches moved. The buck had put his head down behind the log. Daniel waited for a few seconds, hoping the buck would lift his head back up for a shot. When he didn't, Daniel moved one step to his left. As he did, his foot stepped on and snapped a small branch. The sound was all the crafty buck needed. He exploded from his bed and charged headlong into the thick trees away from Daniel. Branches crashed and an avalanche of snow fell from the branches of the trees he brushed by. In an instant, the buck was gone.

Daniel was very disappointed in himself. Yet, he really had no chance for a decent shot. He waited for a couple of minutes, listening for any sounds of the buck. All he could hear was the plopping sound of the falling snow and the pounding of his own heart. He decided to trail the buck for a little while to see if there was some slim chance he might sneak up on him.

Following the buck's tracks was harder than he thought, the snow falling off the trees tended to obliterate them. Still, with patience, he managed to stick with the trail. He was so intent on tracking the buck, that he suddenly realized he had lost his sense of time and direction. How long had he been following the buck's trail? Which direction did he need to go to get to the blockers? It was very hard to tell in the tall, thick trees. Of course, he knew he could follow his own tracks back to where he started, but that would take a long time.

He was starting to feel embarrassed and a little scared, when a whistle startled him from his thoughts. He was extremely glad to see Dale emerge from the trees.

"You saw him, didn't you?"

Daniel excitedly told him what had happened, including how disappointed he was with himself.

"Don't feel bad, Daniel. Those old bucks are pretty smart. Besides, don't give up yet, I've got a plan. Often, deer will circle around when they're being trailed. So here's what I want you to do, follow your tracks back about a hundred yards or so. Find a nice spot where you can watch your back trail. Wait for me there. I'm going to follow old Blackie's trail and just see if he circles around. Maybe I can force him into making a mistake." Dale winked at him and gave him one of his crooked smiles. Then he moved off into the pines.

The way Dale moved so quietly and so easily through the trees reminded Daniel of the mountain men he had read about. Dale always did the hardest part of the walking, yet he never complained and never seemed tired.

Daniel followed his own tracks backwards until he found a spot that he liked. He moved off the trail a few yards, wiped the snow off an old stump and settled down to wait. The trees were a little thinner here, so he could see better than in the real thick stuff. He hoped he would have an opportunity for a better shot. He took off his gloves and put them in his pocket. It had warmed up a lot, so his hands shouldn't get too cold.

He tried to be as still, and as quiet as possible, knowing that any sound or movement might alert the wary buck. Most of the snow had melted off the trees now, so his movement would be much more obvious.

He waited about fifteen minutes without seeing or hearing anything suspicious, when he detected a slight movement in the trees about fifty yards to his left. He was pretty sure it was a deer, but he had no idea if it was the black-horned buck or not. Daniel kept the muzzle of his rifle pointed into the air as he slipped the safety to the off position.

Suddenly, he saw it again; the body of a deer as it glided through the trees. This time, Daniel spied an antler! It had to be the black-horned buck. The animal was moving up the hill toward the top of Respirator Ridge. Daniel brought his rifle up to his shoulder, hoping to get a better look at the deer. Still, the trees prevented him from clearly identifying the buck. Soon, he would be in the very thick trees, and would be impossible to see at all.

"Shoot, Daniel! It's him." Dale's voice echoed through the trees a hundred yards to the buck's rear. The deer seemed to freeze momentarily at the sound of the voice.

Daniel frantically leveled the cross hairs on the buck's midsection, just behind the shoulder, and squeezed the trigger. Kaboom! He hardly felt the rifle's recoil as he quickly worked the Browning's bolt to load another shell. Daniel struggled to locate the buck through his scope again. He could hear the sound of the deer crashing through the trees, heading rapidly for the top of the ridge, but couldn't find him through the heavy underbrush. Should he shoot again? He knew that it was not only useless, but dangerous as well, so he put the safety back on and waited.

Dale arrived within a couple of minutes, sweat was dripping off his face. By that time, all sound of the buck had disappeared over the top of the ridge.

"Did you get him, Dan?" Dale asked.

Daniel shrugged his shoulders. "I don't know. He was in the trees and he didn't hold still for very long."

"Let's go see. Where was he when you shot?" Daniel pointed and Dale lined up with the path of the bullet. "You stay here and tell me when I get to the right spot." He moved off in the direction of Daniel's shot.

Marvin D. Braun

By the time Daniel reached him, Dale had already found out what had happened. "I'm afraid I have some bad news for you Dan. Do you see this branch?" He pointed to a pine branch two inches in diameter. Half of the branch was blown away by a bullet hole. "It looks like you just grazed him." Dale shook his head knowingly. "I found just a little patch of hair that the bullet tore off, but almost no blood. We'll trail him to make sure, but it looks like this branch deflected your bullet just enough to make you miss."

He and Dale followed the black-horned bucks tracks up to the top of Respirator Ridge, searching carefully for any sign that the deer had been wounded. They looked for twenty minutes and found no indication that Daniel's shot had done any real damage. Finally, Dale put his arm around Daniel's shoulders and declared, "I'm sorry, Dan, I know you're disappointed, but there's always tomorrow." He winked and grinned. "We'd better get back to the others. Since I never miss, and you never miss, after hearing your shot, they probably think we bagged him."

They hadn't gone too far when they met Robert and Daniel's father coming up the draw.

Robert spoke. "Thought we'd come and help you drag him down. We heard the shot."

They continued walking down the draw as Daniel told them all that had happened. When he was done, Father responded, "That's part of what makes deer hunting so fun. Deer are such worthy adversaries. It's not getting the big buck that's important, it's the privilege and the challenge to try."

When they got back to the others, Daniel had to retell the story several times. No one seemed to mind that he didn't get the buck, they just seemed impressed and excited that he had actually seen the legendary black-horned buck.

The group road-hunted on the way home and then spent the evening eating steaks and playing cards. Daniel was so tired, he went to bed by nine o'clock. The last thing he remembered thinking about before he drifted off to sleep was a vision of the black-horned buck disappearing across the top of Respirator Ridge.

Marvin D. Braun

Suddenly, the deer came into focus, and for a brief instant, Daniel could see a beautiful set of black antlers.

Chapter 12
The Big Old Ugly

Daniel was extremely tired when Father woke him the next morning. His muscles ached from the rigorous climb up Respirator Ridge yesterday. He guessed everyone else was feeling the same way, because they didn't seem to be in as big of hurry getting started as the first two days.

"There will be more hunters out today since it's Saturday," Clyde remarked, as he took a sip of his coffee. He and Lee had arrived a few minutes earlier.

"This area right along the road might be pretty saturated. Maybe we should go back in a little deeper this morning. What do you think, Robert, how about trying the Big Old Ugly?"

"Now, Clyde," Todd commented, "you shouldn't talk about your brother, Lee, that way. He can't help the way he looks." As always, he hooted loudly at the joke.

Lee grinned and tossed a doughnut at Todd, narrowly missing him. Todd quickly picked up the doughnut and crammed the whole thing in his mouth, as if Lee's toss had hit him there. He was hard to understand as he spoke with the pastry in his mouth. "Now look what you've done, I won't be able to talk for minutes."

The room erupted in cheers and claps. When they were done, Robert answered Clyde's question. "Good idea, Clyde. The hunting pressure from here may drive a few of the bigger bucks that way."

When everyone was done getting ready, they loaded into the vehicles. The weather was chilly and the snow that was left on the ground made a crunching noise when you stepped on it.

"Why do you call this hill the Big Old Ugly?" Daniel asked. Before anyone could answer, he quickly added, "Todd, I don't want you to answer that." Everybody chuckled, then Father answered, "Wait until you see it, Dan. It really is a great big ugly hill. A lot of it is bare and rocky, but there's a strip of pine trees right along the top that deer love to hang out in."

"Is there a chance the Black-Horned Buck might be there?"

"I doubt it. Generally, whitetails stay within a four square-mile area, and the Big Old Ugly is farther away than that."

Marlin continued, "Most hunters think that when there's a lot of hunting pressure, that deer move completely out of the area. Usually, though, they stay right in the territory they're familiar with. The reason you don't see them, is because they stop moving around during the day. They become nocturnal, which means they only move at night. During the day, they stay hidden."

"I imagine," Father added, "that Old Blackie is still somewhere around Big Black Buck Draw. Only now, he'll be even smarter yet."

"I read an article in one of my hunting magazines where they put radio collars on bucks to track their movements while they were being hunted. Often, hunters passed within ten yards of a buck and never saw him."

It took thirty minutes to get to the Big Old Ugly, and by the time they did, Daniel was so turned around in his directions, that he didn't know which direction was which. Todd must have felt the same way, because he remarked, "Looks like my compass is on the fritz again, keeps telling me the wrong direction is north."

Lee quickly asked, "Anybody have a doughnut?" The group laughed quietly.

Lee continued, "Last year, I saw the biggest Black Hills deer I've ever seen on this drive. I hope he's still here."

"There's Big Old Ugly, Daniel." Clyde pointed to a large uneven hill just ahead. "The walkers get to climb all the way up this side of it. Then they flush out that strip of trees right up on top."

Robert's pickup stopped ahead of them, and he and Dale got out and came back to Clyde's suburban. Robert spoke, "We need two more guys to walk this with us. Blockers have the best chance at getting a shot. Marlin, you and Clyde already have your bucks. How about you two come with us? Lee, you've done this hunt a number of times, can you get the blockers into position?"

Lee nodded his head yes, and Robert continued, "We'll give you about fifteen minutes before we start up the hill."

Clyde drove the suburban another half mile around the base of Old Ugly. The road gradually curved to the right. On the left hand side of the trail was a grassy meadow. On the right hand side of the road was a band of pine trees. Daniel could see that the trees only went a little ways, and then the hillside was bare except for rocks and an occasional dead stump jutting up here and there.

Lee commented, "The first blocker should get out here. Find a place to sit on the other side of the trees. When the walkers flush them out of the woods up on top, the deer generally head toward these trees to get into some cover. Dick, you want to take this spot?"

"Sure, good luck to the rest of you."

"Same to you. We'll drop Dan off about one hundred yards down the road, and the rest of us will just keep dropping off until we've got this place surrounded."

Father gave them the thumbs up. He began moving into the trees as the suburban drove away.

"Good luck, young 'un." Lee spoke as he stopped the vehicle. Daniel grinned and got out. He loaded a shell into the chamber of his rifle and put it on safe. Then he walked through the trees. What snow was left on the ground still made a lot of noise when you stepped on it, so it would be difficult sneaking up on a deer today. He found a fallen log to sit on. When standing, he could just barely see his father's blaze-orange cap. When sitting down, he was out of sight. This was more like the deer hunting they did back

Daniel and the Black Horned Buck

home in Tripp County. At least, you could see farther than just a few feet.

A group of crows had nested in the trees all around him. As they began waking up, they kept making annoying 'cawing' sounds as they called back and forth to each other. They seemed upset by his intrusion. Daniel was tempted to blast one particularly loud one that was sitting on a branch not far from him, but decided that the shot could spook any deer that might be around. Besides, the crows weren't really doing anything wrong, they were just being stupid crows. He could imagine how crazy they would act if he had Dougy's cat with him.

Once he stopped moving around, the crows settled down and eventually the entire flock flew off. It was a relief to have the irritating noise gone. By now, he figured the walkers should be at the summit of Big Old Ugly.

Suddenly, he noticed movement at the top of the hill. Wow, a whole herd of deer were hustling down the hillside right at him. Daniel hurried to get his scope up to see if any had antlers. As they got closer he could see them well enough without his scope. There were a dozen deer in all, mainly does and a few half-grown fawns.

Several passed on either side of him. One of the fawns stopped within twenty feet and stared back up the hill. It was apparently looking for its mother, because it bleated several times. To Daniel, it sounded about like a baby lamb. The fawn sighted him and curiously approached within a few yards until it caught his scent, then it was gone in a flash.

To his left he heard a shot, and then another. The sound echoed loudly off the surrounding hills. One of their guys must have seen a buck. His adrenal increased as he waited for the possibility of a shot himself. Then he spotted a deer moving cautiously down the hillside, not in a dead run like the last twelve.

Father had told him, "Daniel, after you've hunted deer long enough, you instinctively can tell a buck from a doe, even if you can't see its antlers."

This had to be a buck. Daniel brought his rifle to his shoulder and eyed the deer through his scope. It was a buck, and a nice one too! Daniel couldn't tell exactly how many points, because he couldn't get a clear look at its antlers. The deer kept skirting carefully from one dead tree or boulder to another, never stopping in one place for more than a few seconds at a time. He wasn't sure if it was his imagination or not, but the antlers did seem to be a darker color.

The deer was getting closer now, but still, never gave him a chance for a decent look or shot. Daniel decided that whether it was the Black-Horned Buck or not, the animal was worth harvesting. Daniel's thumb eased the rifle's safety to the off position, ready for the first opportunity of a kill-shot. Without warning, the buck sensed he was in danger, and abruptly swiveled to its left. He raced at top speed away from Daniel…and right towards Father. Kaboom!

Daniel waited impatiently. He wanted to go see if Father had gotten the deer, but knew he had to wait until the blockers arrived. He also knew that Father wouldn't immediately go look at the buck either. Father usually killed his deer with the first shot. He always immediately reloaded and got the deer back in his sights, just in case a humane second shot was needed.

Finally, he saw Marlin emerge from the trees at the top of the hill. Daniel waved to him, unloaded his rifle, and walked quickly towards Father. Dick was already examining the fallen five-by-five. As Daniel got closer, he spoke. "I don't believe it, Daniel. But, I'm willing to bet that this deer is one of the Black-Horned Buck's offspring. Look how dark his horns are, too!"

"Nice buck, Dad," Daniel said. He was relieved that the deer wasn't **the** Black-Horned Buck, but was very happy that his father had harvested such a nice deer. "You must have made a good shot, too. The last I saw him, he was on a dead run."

"True, but he wasn't very far away. I think he sensed you and came right towards me."

As Marlin arrived, he was beaming. "All right, Dick, good job. I think somebody over there must have got one too."

They worked together field-dressing the buck. Gutting a deer still made Daniel a little queasy, but not as bad as the first couple of times he had helped do it.

Daniel and the Black Horned Buck

When finished, they dragged the buck to the road, and waited for the others to pick them up.

As they drove up, everyone looked quite happy, and for a good reason. Lee had bagged the nicest deer of his life. It was apparently the large buck he had seen last year, only this year, it was even bigger. Now, it had matured into a nice-sized six-by-five.

Everyone congratulated Lee and Dick as they compared the size, configuration and color of the two buck's racks. The whitetail that Dick had shot definitely had darker colored antlers than those of Lee's deer. They stood around talking until Dale spoke, "Let's go, we're burning daylight. I'm sure Daniel still has hopes of bagging Old Grampa Blackie. Are you ready Dan?"

"I sure am, Dale."

"Good, let's do the Green Shack Hunt, and then we'll have just enough time for one more drive down Big Black Buck Draw."

Todd groaned. "Yeah, and that means one more merciless hike up Respirator Ridge. I'm going to need all the energy I can get."

Marvin D. Braun

"Me, too," responded Dale. "I'm hungry. Anybody got anything to eat?"

"Well," answered Ken, "you could always ask Marlin for some M & M's."

Chapter 13

The Surprise

Next, the group did a hunt they called The Green Shack Hunt. On top of the ridge that the hunters blocked, was a dilapidated, wooden shack. It was green, because at one time, the wood had been covered with green-colored tar-paper. None of Daniel's group knew if it had been a miner's shelter, or if some hunter had built it as a deer blind.

Both Dale and Robert had a chance to shoot respectable bucks during the drive, but they let them

Marvin D. Braun

go. Father explained to Daniel, "These guys are from Rapid City. They don't want to fill their tags the first weekend, unless it's a fantastic trophy buck. They love to hunt so much that they'd rather save their tags and hunt for a while. This Black Hills season is open for a whole month."

After lunch, they made another drive down Big Black Buck Draw. This time, Daniel was a blocker, and he even got to sit on Big Black Buck Rock. All the snow was melted now, and it was a beautiful warm day. The forest air smelled fresh and clean. With the sunshine shining through the trees, he felt drowsy as he waited for the walkers. It would have been nice to lay back on Big Black Buck Rock and take a nap, but he figured that's exactly when the Black-Horned Buck would sneak by.

Despite his efforts to stay awake, he must have dozed off. Suddenly, he was jolted awake by the sound of crunching leaves. A buck was trotting down the path, and if it stayed on the trail, it would pass within a few feet of his position!

Daniel brought up his rifle and located the deer through his scope. It had a decent rack, but, to his disappointment, it wasn't the Black-Horned Buck. His thumb slipped off the safety and he took aim. The buck was close enough now to make it an easy shot. He kept the cross-hairs trained on the whitetails vital area for several seconds, then decided not to shoot. The buck was decent, but he'd be even better next year.

Daniel sat very still. If the buck stayed on the path, the breeze would keep Daniel's scent from reaching him. The animal was so intent on getting down the trail, that it didn't even notice him as he passed by within ten feet.

Daniel was proud of himself. It was a good feeling knowing that he had given the buck a second chance. By next year, the deer would be a much smarter adversary. That was part of what made deer hunting such a great sport.

It was their final drive for this year's hunt. Afterwards, they went back to the cabin and played cards, pool, and gorged themselves on Uncle Marlin's elk chislic. It was delicious.

The trip home was pretty uneventful. Daniel slept part of the way because he was so tired from all the walking while deer hunting, and from staying up late playing cards. Of course, the group stopped at Wall Drug for their free doughnut.

Daniel used his own money to buy some doughnuts to take home for Dougy, Angie, and mother. He also bought Dougy a large whistling tube that sounded like an elk bugling when you twirled it. He was sure everyone at home, and especially the cat, would appreciate it. He also bought some arrow heads for the upcoming Tripp County deer hunt. He hoped he could play the same trick on Uncle Ralph, Mitch, and Vern (see <u>Daniel's First Deer Hunt</u>), that Ken had played on Dale and Marlin.

Six months after the Black Hills deer hunt, Daniel received a package in the mail. From the post mark, he could tell it was from Rapid City. He opened the letter attached to the outside of the package and it said:

Dear Daniel,

   I found these while looking for shed antlers up on Respirator Ridge two weeks ago. You deserve them as much as anybody.

Your friend,

Dale

P.S. I guess it means old Blackie is still out there.

   As Dougy looked on, Daniel quickly tore open the box to see what it contained. Inside were two deer antlers, each with five points, and both were almost black.

The End

Marvin D. Braun

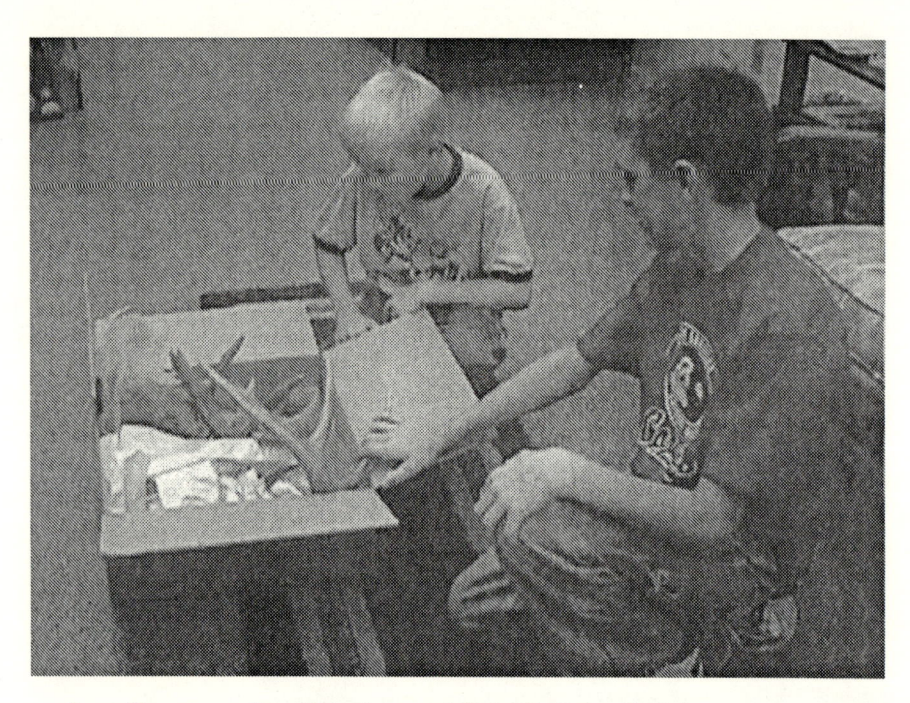

As Dougy looked on, Daniel quickly tore open the box to see what it contained. Inside were two deer antlers, each with five points, and both were almost black.

About the Author

Marvin Braun is an avid hunter who loves the outdoors. He is the author and originator of the "Daniel" hunting books, a series of first chapter books that teach valuable lessons about safe, ethical hunting.

Printed in the United States
1535500005B/303